# The Black Beacon Book of Pirates

OTHER TITLES FROM BLACK BEACON BOOKS

Anthologies:

*The Black Beacon Book of Horror*
*The Black Beacon Books of Mystery*
*Tales from the Ruins*
*A Hint of Hitchcock*
*Murder and Machinery*
*Shelter from the Storm*
*Lighthouses*
*Subtropical Suspense*

Collections:

*Oscar Tremont, Investigator of the Strange and Inexplicable*
*The Animal Inside*
*Hoffman's Creeper and Other Disturbing Tales*
Cameron Trost

*Dark Reflections*
Paul Kane

Novels:

*Flicker*
*Letterbox*
*The Tunnel Runner*
Cameron Trost

*Fortitude*
*Courage*
Karen Bayly

**www.blackbeaconbooks.com**

*the*

# BLACK BEACON BOOK

*of*

# PIRATES

*The Black Beacon Book of Pirates*
Published by Black Beacon Books
Edited by Cameron Trost
Cover art by Daniele Serra (The Long Journey)
Copyright © Black Beacon Books, 2024

*The Mutineer* © Lawrence Dagstine
*The End of All Tides* © Paulene Turner
*Poll Pirate* © Michael Fountain
*The Ghost* © Bailey W. Stutzman (S. B. Watson)
*And the Sea* © Jack Wells
*Dungeon Rock* © Edward Lodi
*The Avery Dog Has His Day* © Rose Biggin
*The Curse of the Emerald Eye* © Cameron Trost
*Les Femmes Sauvages* © Karen Bayly
*Sting of the Schorpioen* © David-John Tyrer (DJ Tyrer)
*Beholden to No One* © Karen Keeley

Black Beacon Books
blackbeaconbooks.com

ISBN: 9780645247183

Hidden treasure, ancient curses, mythical sea creatures, uncharted waters, and rip-roaring adventure across the seven seas—The Black Beacon Book of Pirates carries a clandestine cargo of timber-shivering, plank-walking, and swashbuckling goodies. You'll be entertained by tall tales of yore recounted over the drunken din in the dingiest of taverns, you'll embark upon the most perilous of undertakings on the high seas, and you'll be reminded that even today, the legacy of pirates and privateers of a bygone age follows our every step like a shadow—but wait, what's that behind you? It's too dark to be a mere shadow...and what's that in its hand? No, not *in* its hand, but *instead of* a hand! A steely hook ready to strike! There's only one way to escape. Turn the page and set sail! This book is your helm. If you stick to it and hold fast, you might just make it back to port alive, me hearty!

*- Cameron Trost, editor*

Black Beacon Books would like to thank our patrons, whose passion for great fiction and independent publishing helped make this anthology happen.

If you'd like to join the team and reap the benefits, subscribe on our Patreon page at: *patreon.com/blackbeaconbooks*

The five patronage tiers are
*Shipwreck Survivor, Moonlight Smuggler, Sea Witch, Assistant Keeper,* and *Lighthouse Keeper.*

**Author Biographies**

# THE MUTINEER

## Lawrence Dagstine

It was late in the evening before Father Martim, a pious man with a potbelly and jovial disposition, worked his way around to me. But this particular night he wasn't his genial self. I remembered our talk together in the Caribbean Straits. 'It looks,' I said ruefully, 'as though the only name I've made for myself is not founded in swashbuckling heroics but that of a mutinous fool.'

His face was gray with exhaustion as he laid a hand on my shoulder. 'You have chosen your path, Frederick March the Third,' he said. 'Look for no reward this side of heaven. As time passes the journey in unto itself shall become clearer to you.' Then he gave me absolution.

For a while the bread and wine afforded a glow of almost physical comfort. I felt exalted. As a pirate, I was, I told myself, dying for honor and loyalty. As the night wore on, however, I gave way to despair. If only, I thought, I had the same decision to make again. My lord, a quartermaster and swordfish sailor by trade, would think none the worse of me if I saved myself. Quite possibly faced with the prospect of a razor-sharp guillotine, my head would serve no justice on the chopping block. My death would surely bring no benefit to him.

The hours passed slowly, but I must have dozed off, for I remember waking with a start to a sudden flood of light. The hatch at the top of the stairs was unbattened, and we were hauled to our feet. It was dawn.

There were about a dozen of us, and we were marched to the shore to the beat of a funeral drum. The ships' companies were drawn up to form three sides of a square; on the fourth side were gibbets and blocks. It was sleeting, clouds were low over the hills, and I realized

9

that I had looked my last on blossom, sun and the love-bright eyes of a dockhand's fair maiden.

The captain general's voice was hard and adamant. 'I command you all to step forward!'

I would have liked to answer with dignity. Instead, I spat at the captain general in defiance. 'Cut off his head yourself,' I screamed. 'Filthy murderer!'

I could see he was angry, but he controlled his voice and let his glance travel slowly down the line of condemned men. 'I cannot believe,' he said quietly, 'that *all* of you wish to betray the Monarchy and *all* of you wish to die. I swear by the Virgin Mary that he who is first to step forward to sever this traitor's head shall go forth a free man.'

For a moment there was much shifting of feet and exchanging of glances. I couldn't bring myself to watch as they cut off my lord's head. All I could think of was the way he had held me close in the Sea of Souls, like the father I had never known, as he had carried this young boy swabbing decks to his cabin. He taught me how to properly use a compass, steer a boat with one oar, turn a ship with a flimsy sail inward during a hurricane, how to handle a dagger, the seaman's usual tools of the trade. I knew when he died because a great sigh rose like a benediction, hung for a moment in the morning air, then merged into the roar of breakers along the shore. I think my childhood died with him.

The captain general shook his head. 'All we wanted was the boatswain, and you buffoons couldn't even get that right.'

What happened next was anticlimax. They drew and quartered the old seafarer I nicknamed granddad and hoisted the remains of him alongside a long half-sinking pier of starving seagulls, the most ravenous of their kind I had ever seen.

The remaining lot of us were lucky. We had been given the most precious gift of all: *life*. Yet in the months that followed we sometimes almost regretted it. For in charge of our chain gangs was Mephisto, a taskmaster cruel and cold as the blizzards that swept down from Greenland's Alps.

It is hard to find words sufficiently bleak to describe that winter up north. The setting was somber: gray cliffs, gray sky, gray waves pounding without respite against a drab gray shore. On three days out of four a cold mist drifted in from the sea, like nothing we'd ever felt; on the fourth a raw biting wind blew off the hills, bringing flurries of snow. As prisoners, we had been relocated to this small seaside tundra that I liked to call Arctic Hell. Our taskmasters had the luxury of donning yak furs and filling their rotund bellies with warm mead, while we were half starved, half naked. We unloaded stores and careened the ships, often up to our waists in icy water.

Yet all of this would have been bearable if it hadn't been for the silence. This was Mephisto's most vindictive punishment. While at work we spoke no word. The only sounds were the clink of chains, the pound of waves and the dolorous cries of the seabirds. There was another factor too to dampen our spirits—the gibbets, and the things I couldn't bring myself to look at which swung from them. Evidence, for those who still needed any, that the captain general was not a man to be trifled with.

We had plenty of time to think, that harsh northern winter of 1605, and I began to ask myself questions. For example, why was the crew now treating me with a new respect? With ink and quill in hand, I reckoned I should keep a diary of events before bed every night—how this all came about to begin with. Obviously because I had refused to act as my lord's executioner. But also because of a cosmic horror of a man, known as the boatswain. The captain general had spent half his life, on behalf of the Monarchy, traveling from one ocean to the next, in search of this seafaring aberration which was said to have eight ethereal tentacles protruding from its back. Some brigands said he was the human manifestation of Dagon himself; others insisted he was some ill portent which doomed many a pirate along the spice routes. If the boatswain caught you and wrapped its tentacles around you, it could suck the very essence of your life force out of you. So the story goes. You would then shrivel up into a husk and die mercilessly at his feet. This was how the boatswain fed on his victims, and the captain general guaranteed the Monarchy that he would seize this absolute power, bring it back to the throne and help thy kingdom harness it. Empty promises, if you ask me.

But I can tell you firsthand. I have *met* the boatswain. I have come face to face with this entity. He dresses one part the quartermaster yet the other part the fisherman in rubbers, wears an executioner's hood to conceal his face, walks on water when the need arises, and

11

carries a rusty fish hook in his right hand. The tales about his tentacles are true. He has eight of them, sticking out of his spine, four to each side, and they are quite luminescent on a clear night in the light of a full moon. And he let me *live*.

It was in the Atlantic, along a series of uncharted isles. The water always became steeper when circling these regions, the head wind so strong that in the violent squalls which came up without warning we were often blown backward. Our passage down these desolate coasts, guarded by sharp reefs and scoured by a thirty-foot tide, was made even more perilous by the captain general's insistence that we stand close in to every inlet in the hope it would prove the entrance to Hades, the supposed whirlpool-like lair of the boatswain.

But Hades' existence was as elusive as a rainbow's end. Week after week we clawed into the eye of the wind, our storm canvas split, and our decks almost continuously awash. My lord retired to his cabin, muttering of the perils we were led into. He took little interest in handling the ship. This was perhaps as well, since he was getting too old to be a sailor and on the one occasion he did intervene he was the cause of one and very nearly five deaths, including my own. But I still loved him. How couldn't I?

Saltwater had seeped into our casks and turned meat and fish putrid. He requested permission from the other ships to put a foraging party ashore. That next afternoon, as our armada explored a skein of islands which for once was sunlit and serene, I could sense rebellion simmering. He swung out of line and dropped anchor in the lee of a bay. 'Lower the longboat,' my lord ordered. He called for volunteers to be put ashore and the first mate selected five, including myself. 'Don't come back without the boatswain.' To me, he handed his finest scimitar. 'I polished it myself, boy. Go ahead. It's yours now.' He turned around. 'And to the first man that brings me those tentacles, you will eat of the finest roast beef money can buy and the sweetest ale you can guzzle down. All on the Monarchy's coin. And bring some geese back with you. They too will make a fine feast.'

It was too irresistible to pass up. Our first difficulty though was the riptide. It ran like a millrace, so that we found ourselves swept past the beach we had picked for landing and onto a more rugged part of the shore. Eventually, however, watched by a solemn concourse of our victims-to-be, we struggled onto a slab-like protuberance of rock and hauled up the longboat. The gosling showed no fear, even when we began to lay into them with our clubs, but waited with an air of polite surprise for the blows that split their skulls. In next to no time, we had killed enough to meet our needs and were dragging the carcasses to the shore.

Suddenly the toothy grunt with no tongue beside me straightened up with an exclamation of surprise. Hitherto the evening sky had been devoid of malice. Now a copper-colored cloud was pouring out from behind the mountains. Almost at once the gold of the sunset was metamorphosed to a sepulchral gloom, an ice-cold wind began to slam in wayward gusts, and little waves came surging up the shore.

'The path to Hades opens up!' shouted the oarsman. 'What omen befalls us?'

'Look lively when loading up,' the first mate hollered back at him. 'Be ready for anything. Understand? Anything.'

It took us no more than a couple of minutes to haul the last of the carcasses aboard the longboat, but in those five minutes a great squall came sweeping over the island. Within the center of the squall, something was visible. A man—no!—something *else*. Tentacles lashed out and knocked me clean off my feet and, passing into the bay, tipped the longboat so that her yardarm dipped into the sea. We thought she must surely turn turtle, but somehow she managed to right herself. Then she ran for it, clawing away from a lee shore to the comparative safety of open water.

'Look out!' yelled the oarsman, falling backwards in the sand. Two more tentacles shot out at us from the center of the squall. One lashing out from the left, followed by a lengthy right jab.

It was some moments before the truth of our predicament struck home. We were marooned with the boatswain slowly closing in on us. And geese. Lots of dead geese.

Suddenly the squall disappeared. Waves of water that had been levitating seconds earlier as if by some arcane arts now hit the ground with a loud splash.

'He'll be back for us when the storm blows itself out.' The first mate's words were discomforting, and he was not altogether successful in keeping the fear from his eyes.

'Then we'd better get back to the ship,' I said.

'Not that simple, I'm afraid. It's a long way out.'

We were wondering what to do next when an even more violent hammer blow of wind bludgeoned us to our knees, making us cling like limpets to the rocks.

'He's in the wind, he's in the wind!' shouted the oarsman.

'No. He's coalescing with the water,' said another grunt. 'He must be. It's the only explanation.'

I forced myself to my feet and took in the scene. At first I could hardly believe what my eyes beheld—the longboat nestled on the rocks.

'Look there!' I shouted, pointing at the vessel. 'She must have been washed back when the water came crashing down. Don't we have that big fishing net?'

'What about it?' said the first mate.

'We can use it to capture him. The net should be strong enough to keep his tentacles at bay.'

'The boat!' I sensed rather than heard the cry of dismay. The sea had risen so swiftly that waves were creaming white round its stern, each backwash threatening to suck it free of the rocks. We hurried down and struggled with it to a place of high waterline, where a miniature gully gave shelter from the worst of wind and spray. 'This ravine,' I said. 'It'll have to do.' Here we retrieved the net and tipped the longboat onto its side, a makeshift bivouac, and temporary protection from the tentacles lashing out at us.

Trembling with cold, we huddled together in the lee of the upended boat and waited for the wind to die down. The wind, however, increased in fury—the work of the boatswain, no doubt—and soon the darkness of night was added to the darkness of the storm, with the wind a constant high-pitched shriek, snow scything out of the sky, and cold more biting than any I had ever known.

'We can't stay hidden beneath these rocks forever,' said the oarsman. 'He'll find us, you know. He's the one causing this, with those glowing feelers of his.'

'He could have killed us up on the beach when he had the chance,' I said.

'What do you mean?' asked the first mate.

'What if this boatswain is trying to keep us out of harm's way? What if he is using those tentacles of his to manipulate the weather, snap the storm and sleet back away from us?'

As the gusts settled, I realized it was the boatswain who had saved our lives. With his rusty hook pointing down from an outcropping of dense rock and a downed coconut tree, he bade us turn the boat keel into the winds and pile stones either side of its stern so it was anchored even and fast. Then he spread his tentacles wide out and shined light down upon us, and the pools of radiance threw the internal ribs of the longboat into weird relief, making it seem as though we were imprisoned, like Jonah, in the stomach of some prehistoric whale. Finally, he made us slap our arms and flex our legs. 'No one must sleep,' he warned us, his voice reverberating like an echo on the wind, 'lest the blood congeal in his body.'

As the night wore on, the temperature dropped still further. By midnight we began to shiver in great spasms, like men in the grip of fatigue. Our hands and feet started to lose every vestige of feeling. I looked at my companions, slumped half-conscious against the ribs of the boat, with the breath condensing to ice on their beards. It came to me that we were dying of exposure to the elements.

'Wake up!' The boatswain's voice seemed to come from a long way off. 'The gosling...they'll keep you warm... If you kill enough, you can bury yourselves in the bodies, make the journey back to your armada.'

It seemed a mad idea at the time. I remember struggling to hone my knife with fingers numb from frostbite, and the breath near freezing in my throat as we emerged from the shelter of the boat. Then I took my lord's scimitar in hand. With a hacking and slashing motion I got to work. The blade was much easier to handle than your average cut-throat's dagger. I remember the powdery snow on the rocks, the moon scudding between great mountain ranges of cloud, and the sudden fish-like stench as we stumbled into a colony of geese. Then we were dragging the avian carcasses back, just as the boatswain had instructed us. Inside the upended boat the five of us felt like Vikings, as we built a great cairn of them, put some kerosene in a dry lantern, and crawled underneath.

'Go back to your captain now,' the boatswain said from the ridge above us. 'And never return to this place.'

The stench was like that of a charnel house, so overpowering that one of the deckhands, retching and coughing, declared he would rather die of exposure than bury himself in a dunghill of still-warm bodies. He crawled from the mound of gosling and wedged himself in the stern. The rest of us were not so squeamish. I bored myself into the mass of geese, feathers everywhere, covering all my body with theirs, feeling the life-giving warmth of them slowly restore my circulation for the journey back. My drowsiness now was not the sleep of death but the sleep of life, and I nestled into the dark warmth. All thanks to the boatswain, an aberration we had set out to destroy.

I woke the next morning sick, dizzy and short of air, with foul mouth and splitting head. But alive.

The first mate covered his mouth, belched and said, 'I think I'm going to puke.' He looked over at me. 'Why do you think he spared us?'

'I don't think he ever intended to harm us,' I said honestly.

'So, he just didn't want us intruding on his isle?'

'Something along those lines. The captain general might know more than he is letting on. Same goes with the ministers in the Monarchy.'

'So, what must I do to earn myself a name now?' asked the grunt to my left.

'Be patient,' I answered. 'And when you become a full-fledged swashbuckler, a name will be given you, according to the type of pirate you have become.'

There is little point in chronicling all we went through in our voyage back to the armada. Another storm, another night in a boat which reeked of dead gosling: thirst, hunger, frostbite, and the sickness that comes from drinking rainwater mingled with seawater. Indeed, we were all alive—all, that is, except the toothy fellow who had risked exposure. His clothing stiff with rime, he was practically frozen like a white skeleton. But he had suffered parasites before we set out. We promised to bury him as best we could, perhaps in one of the rare oases of shingle you find along solace shores, perhaps in a glade or wilderness of barnacled rock.

We were close to the end of our tether now when, late on the second afternoon, the oarsman gave a cry of exultation. 'A sail! A sail!'

And there, God be praised, heeled over under a great press of sail, was a carrack and my lord, standing sun-bronzed and smiling in the

16

rays of a new day's sun, staring handsomely into the bay. It was a sight for sore eyes.

We launched ourselves into position and rowed for the carrack, little caring that our muscles ached and our oars seemed weighted with lead.

We had twenty-four hours after we got back to recuperate, then the captain general sent a messenger to our ship to tell us he wanted to see us and, to my lord in private, after learning we came back empty-handed, that the Monarchy had no room for idle hands.

#

In the coming months up north, I sought guidance from Father Martim. 'I was right, wasn't I, to refuse to kill my lord?'

His answer wasn't quite what I expected. 'There are some decisions, Frederick, that a man must arrive at alone, with his conscience, without being told "This is right" or "This is wrong".'

At that same moment Mephisto pounded on the prison door. 'Put down your diary, prisoner! You have fifteen minutes. Then I want you back in your shackles cutting ice with the other scalawags.'

'So,' I asked the priest eagerly, knowing I had very little free time left to me. 'I am now a man or a mutineer?'

He smiled. 'You remember the time I first met you and your fleet?'

'I think so,' I said. 'Everything is a blur since we left the Caribbean.'

'I told you that if you overcame the three temptations—the world, the flesh, and the devil—you'd be a man indeed. Well, I fancy you've overcome the first.'

I thought it over. 'So, my next task would be to overcome the flesh? How do I do that?'

He laid a hand on my shoulder. 'Be not so impatient, lad, to grow up. All that God ordains shall come to pass.'

But I was conscious of the chains round my feet every day, and the coldness of the wind. Patience, it seemed to me, was a virtue I might not be able to afford.

'What about the devil?' I then asked curiously. 'What if the boatswain was the devil, and that was me getting too far ahead of

17

myself?'

'And what if the captain general is the devil in disguise? What if the boatswain is actually a guardian angel, the product of some higher benevolent power? Lucifer takes on many ruthless forms, my boy.'

'Get out here this instant, March!' Mephisto yelled from the torch-lit, cobblestoned hallway. 'I won't say it again.' The taskmaster was a vicious and barbaric grunt that tolerated no hindrance, neither small nor large. Tardiness was just one of them.

'I better go, Father.'

As winter closed in we began to suffer from exposure and from malnutrition on the traditional prisoners' diet of biscuit and water. We grew pale and emaciated. Where our skins were broken by chain, rock or barnacle, great sores festered. Eventually we became so weak that Mephisto reluctantly agreed to increase our rations. But he ran into an unexpected impasse: more food was not available. We thought at the time that he was inventing an excuse to keep us on short supply. It was only later that we learned what had happened. Instead of the captain general's personal fleet sailing with food for thirty-six months, including reserves, they had sailed with enough for a bare twelve. And most of this, by now, had been used up; this is what happens when you don't give the Monarchy a hundred and ten percent.

'With food for only a few months, it would be madness to go on,' said one prisoner.

'Can't you see the Monarchy is being spiteful to our armada in particular,' said another. 'This is all because we did not bring back the boatswain as intended.'

'We must eke out the winter as best we can,' I muttered. 'Then either return home or head back for the Caribbean, or some other warm climate.'

'Tell that to the captain general,' said the first mate. 'I don't see the Monarchy giving us a pardon anytime soon.'

One afternoon the captain general greeted us most courteously, a mannerism unsuitably reserved for such a scoundrel and which I was sure he had not the slightest intention of keeping. Definitely not for a band of pirates in shackles. 'We shall spend the winter in procuring and salting fresh food: mussels from the estuary, hardskin crab from beneath the frozen lakes, snowy mallards from the rime marshes, gosling from the surrounding islands, the odd seal or albatross, and venison from the hides of walruses themselves. Then in the spring we shall return south. We will embark once more on our quest for the boatswain. Let's hope this time you lot get it right. There may even be a bigger reward this time around.'

#

The voyage that spring was pleasant enough to begin with—for starters, we were no longer wearing shackles or prisoners' leggings—for the sun was warmer than we'd known it the previous six months, and the southern narrows opened out to form a sheltered stretch of water surrounded by grassy hills. We had been pushing forward for about three days in early April, much occupied with sounding, when we sighted a cluster of huts at the water's edge. It was an isle tranquil in beauty, and one we had never discovered.

I looked at the maps made available to us by the Monarchy. 'Definitely uncharted,' I said, navigational tools in hand.

'It shimmers like Atlantis,' said one voyager on deck, his eye glued to his pocket telescope. 'But it is too prehistoric to be Atlantean.'

'Hades then, perhaps,' I said.

'Or some other landlubber's folly,' argued the first mate.

Our armada dropped anchor, and the captain general, who was now our permanent lord, called for a landing party; to me and the first mate he handed a fat purse of doubloons, expecting the most out of us. 'Don't make me regret this,' he muttered. 'There is a lot at stake here. I'm relying on you.' There were ten volunteers, myself leading them. The first mate was in charge of all boat parties, and he had his own volunteers to contend with.

The first thing we noticed as our longboat approached the shore was a curious gray object, like the hulk of a great ship which appeared to be stranded at the water's edge; it was surrounded by a multitude of seabirds. As we neared it, however, we became aware of the most horrible stench. Our strokes shortened and faltered, and finally we drifted to a halt, resting on our oars and staring in amazement at a nauseous scene. For the seabirds, we suddenly

19

realized, were ripping away great ribbons of flesh. The gray object was none other than the carcass of a great monster. So huge was it that I declare if twenty elephants had been placed nose to tail, and probably just as high, they would scarce have reached to the end of it.

'It is Leviathan!'—one of the oarsmen crossed himself—'the oceanic lord himself.'

'No, it is Neptune. His *true* form,' said another, much younger crewmate. 'He washed up mutilated on this beach.'

'It is neither Leviathan nor Neptune,' I hollered. 'Get a grip, would you? Look at the remaining flesh. Those wounds. Tentacles wrapped themselves around this creature. Lots of tentacles. The effort to reel this sea monster in was collaborative. They probably lashed the beast to get it out of the oceanic depths, the deepest of the deep, and keep it at bay. This creature, though mysterious, was hunted. That much is obvious.'

We pulled hastily for the shore. Landing, we headed toward the huts, our scimitars and blunderbusses at the ready. To our surprise there was no sign of life. It was an eerie scene: gray sky, barren landscape, a sea monster murdered just off the beach, and a moaning wind which tingled our senses and made our ears ring.

Perhaps this was Hades after all.

As we neared the deserted huts, we saw they were in fact platforms raised some six feet above the ground and covered with thatch. There seemed to be immobile octopus creatures—half man, half cephalopod—sleeping on each, but as we tiptoed close we saw to our dismay that the sleeping figures were the mummified corpses of ancient oceanic warriors.

Each was close on seven feet in length and appeared to have been smoked over a fire before being coated in ink, pitch, and encased in a burial shroud made from the skins of whales. Round the neck of each man was a string of shells, on his forehead an executioner's hood or skullcap bearing the symbol of an octopus, and by his side a long hardwood spear, a war club studded with sharks' teeth, and a short obsidian knife. And how could I forget the tentacles? Each mummified form had eight tentacles, four to each side, protruding out of the thoracic part of their spines. Only the light of these tentacles was now black as night. They were almost husk-like, the life having died out of them a long time ago.

'These are the same tentacles the captain general told us about,' said a member of the longboat crew. 'Is this the boatswain's people?'

'Very likely,' I said with a nod.

'Is the boatswain here now?' asked a nerve-racked oarsman.

'I don't know,' I replied softly. 'Stay vigilant.'

Glancing at the two dozen or so dead warriors elevated above me, I wondered if this was what Father Martim was referring to months earlier: the temptation of the flesh. Mummification of another's remains. Perhaps it was in reference to the boatswain's tribe all along, if it even was his people. How far off could the temptation of the devil be? And what would Satan himself have in store? Even little old me, often sprite and nimble and full of piss and vinegar, who feared neither God nor man, was shaken; my longboat crew even more so. 'This is no place for us,' I muttered as the burial platforms creaked and swayed in the wind. 'Let us go back to the boat, circle around the island, lest the devil himself come to claim us.'

An hour later we were under way. I for one had no regrets as a sea mammoth's carcass and burial platforms with human octopuses merged into the darkness of the hills. As we stood west, the sun became clearer, the air fresher, and the country on either side became greener and more spectacular, the land giving way to steep mountains covered with beech and pine and laced with cascading waterfalls. At twilight we came to the spot where the sea debouched into a narrow channel, then a lake, the captain general's rumored "place of terror", and here we dropped anchor for the night. The first mate was not far behind with his longboat and crew.

Our passage down the channel proved less hazardous than we had feared, for next morning my party took advantage of a slack tide and a flowing wind. Within a couple of hours the channel's cavernous walls of rocks were behind us, and we had emerged into another and greater lake, which stretched away into a wide circular arc in the distance. We had covered some twenty miles inland when we came to a large round clearing.

'Right here,' I said over my shoulder, standing portside. 'The lake goes no further. Seems peaceful enough, too.'

We disembarked. It was while following this route that my men first sighted the footprints of giants. 'More tentacle people?' one said, touching the ground.

'Could be,' I said, kneeling over one large print.

Or it could have been the boatswain himself, coming in and out of the cove.

The footprints traversed the muddy bank of a lagoon. My longboat crew investigated further. They were deep, wide-spaced and a full cubit from toe to heel. Though my dispatch did their very best to follow the tracks and spent the rest of the day casting about the lagoon, they saw no signs of life.

While we mutineers were turned into trackers and hunters and kept at work ashore, the more prominent members of the crew moved in. Succulent looking seafowl were snared or brought down from their nests with throwing sticks; then they were plucked, smoked, salted and packed into barrels. The gosling were bludgeoned to death with clubs and their bodies put to a great variety of uses: their flesh was eaten, their blubber melted down to provide oil for our lamps, and their pelts sewn together to make jackets and rugs. The venison came from the strange creatures that roamed the forests in great herds: with the head and ears of a mule, the neck and body of a camel, the legs of a stag and the tail of a horse. I know not what else to call it. They were rotund in shape and seemed almost mythical in appearance. But they tasted delicious when pinned over our cook's spit-roast, and with the right mead they made for a fine feast.

We had been there a whole week before we spotted an octopus warrior, quite naked, with tentacles surrounding its tall frame, singing and leaping about on the shore, the while throwing sand and dust over his head. This one was obviously a member of the living. The first mate sent one of his more experienced seamen toward him, charging him to leap and sing in a similar manner as a sign of friendship. And this seaman, behaving as he had been ordered, persuaded the tentacle warrior to follow him. When the warrior saw us, together with our carracks and arms, he pointed to the sky to ask if we came from heaven. He was so tall that the largest of us came not to his shoulder. His eyes were ringed with yellow, on his cheeks were painted two red octopuses, and his hair was scanty and powdered white. Besides the electrified feelers stretching far out from his back, he was armed with a short bow. The arrows, tipped with stone and dipped in some sort of aromatic poison, were stuck in a band round his head.

The captain general now plodded up the beach, one hand on his elegantly designed scabbard the other on his irregularly shaped waist. 'Can't you see this native is restless?' he said, shaking his head in disapproval. 'Don't just stand there. Offer him some meat.' He ordered him to be given food and drink on the spot—preferably alcoholic—and the captain general's subordinates, such as Mephisto, offered him a steel mirror. When the tentacle warrior saw himself in this he was greatly terrified, leaping back and knocking over four of our pirates. As a parting gift we gave him two bells, a comb, some ink and parchment, and a silver rosary from the drawer of one of the ministers of the Monarchy itself.

He returned next morning and led us to the place where he lived and, in turn, the captain general hoped this would lead to the current whereabouts of the boatswain.

About a dozen miles out from our camp, at the foot of a cliff, we found a hut made of wattle and daub, and in it two men and their wives. The women were almost as tall as their spouses, equally tattooed and in headdress, and they too donned eight tentacles which shimmered in the haze of the island sun.

They appeared to have no possessions save earthenware pots, the skins of guanaco and large trout, and tablets etched with caveman-like figures praising some manner of multi-limbed sea god. We assumed the tribe were the Neanderthals in these slate drawings. The rest of the inhabitants were strongly built, standing seven feet in height or above, the males with long muscular arms and legs, the females with enormously long teats. The whole party came back with us to our main vessel, the men walking proudly in front carrying nothing but their bows, the women trailing behind laden like mules.

They stayed with us for several days, during which we were able to learn a little of their customs and beliefs, along with how they cured stomachache by eating thistles to make them vomit; how they cured headache by making great gashes across their foreheads and soaking the wound with the ink of cuttlefish; how they lived on nothing but raw flesh and waterfall algae; and how when they died their bodies were taken over by the devils who guarded the entrance to Hades and the Abyss. Two demons from two very different interpretations of hell, which have horns on their heads, hair down to their feet, breathe tidal waves and belch fire. Supposedly the boatswain was the keeper, a grim reaper-like figure who stood between these two fierce demons. He traversed the narrow channels between Hades and the Abyss, guiding the ethereal remnants of his people to their correct portals. He was the appointed mariner for this tribe to and from the afterlife. All this Father Martim recorded in his diary, and this information would be passed on to the Monarchy when we got back. Eventually they left us, clothed in our shirts, breeches and jerkins, and carrying gifts. Through bribery we had learned a little more about the boatswain each passing day; it was a lot more than we had known before we came ashore.

But it was not enough for the captain general. I could see it in his eyes.

In the weeks to come our relations with the octopus warriors, whom we named Octopoda, were not to stay friendly. About late autumn we came across four more of the Octopoda warriors, who had drifted too far from their village. The captain general decided to capture two of the youngest ones for experimentation by the Monarchy. Perhaps they too possessed the powers of the boatswain. Perhaps it was inherent. Perhaps it was a supernatural ability which coursed through their blood, and had done so for many generations. After all, they all had the same lightning-like feelers. If the captain general couldn't have the boatswain's power, then he would capitalize off the next best thing. This he did by a trick, which the first mate and I did not know about at first. None of the mutineers were aware. They were piling barrels into storage and swabbing the decks of the adjacent vessel when this all took place. First, more bribes. The captain general loaded them with so many gifts—beads, mirrors, scissors and bells—that their hands were full. It didn't help that they were shiny and silver and were appealing. Then he nodded to Mephisto who brought out a pair of fetters and offered them these too. The Octopoda were grieved that their hands were too full to accept the fetters, so Mephisto offered to hang them about their legs.

The captain general whispered in Mephisto's ear, 'Once we have these two locked up where we want them, you bring the baubles to the other two.'

'Will four be enough?' Mephisto asked.

'For now,' the captain general said. 'Until I can get a closer look at those tentacles.'

Not until the trusting young warriors were shackled and forcefully escorted to the brig did they realize they were trapped. Then the captain general had Mephisto take his scimitar and, one by one, hack off their feelers. The tentacles were wrapped up in coarse twine and tossed into a giant supply chest in the steward's chamber. Then the distressed Octopoda, bleeding profusely from their backs, flung themselves this way and that, foaming at the mouth like bulls, and calling on the boatswain for aid. It took a full dozen of the captain general's entourage to restrain them, while we were at work on the armada's other barge.

The morning we sailed, the wind was keen off the pole, and so great was the cold that no sooner had we hoisted anchor than the chains froze solid to the deck. The armada was made up of two vessels now, a main one and a minor one. The supply ships had cast out a month earlier. It seemed to me that once we ventured beyond the archipelago we would be lucky to survive. However, now that we had made enemies of the Octopoda, the captain general wanted to find alternative winter anchorage.

Our slow-moving armada picked its course through skein after skein of islands, each, it seemed, richer and more beautiful than the one before. The light snowfall made things seem more tranquil. Only an unusual fog behind us concerned us, but we were way ahead of its eerie thickness. A couple of times we landed for water, marveling at the proliferation of creatures on the beaches, birds and sea turtles mainly, the odd sea lion here and there.

Then, on the third day out, we saw something catching up to us from the density of the fog. The mass of gloom was thicker than any mist I had ever encountered whilst seafaring abroad, and unspeakable echoes reverberated from the center of this unsettling haze.

'Is that the utterances of the dead?' the first mate asked me.

I looked over the side of the ship, telescope in hand. 'I don't know. Whatever it is, it sounds inhuman.'

'Hell follows on our footsteps,' one of the mast handlers said in fright. 'The Octopoda knows we took what belongs to them. They have sent the boatswain and his demonic legions to fetch what is theirs back!'

'Get back to work, you lowly dogs!' the captain general hollered from the starboard side of the main ship. 'It is just fog, like any other fog. Keep our current course, or you'll find yourselves swimming home!'

In the captain general's success at obtaining tentacles, however, were the seeds of tragedy, for he became filled with such proselytizing zeal that he altogether lost interest in mundane matters such as careening the ships and, most of all, the boatswain.

We anticipated that we would speed back north of the Atlantic, but nothing could have been further from the truth. We had scarce sailed at midday before the wind increased in fury and backed from south to east. Suddenly we were embayed by what is the nightmare of every seaman, with a murky fog on our tail: a lee shore. We had no seaway, and we couldn't claw out of the estuary, for the wind blew directly into it. And we couldn't beat out sideways, for at the end of each tack we were brought up short by the cliffs at the estuary mouth.

By mid-afternoon on the fourth day we found ourselves being driven inexorably backward, into the center of the fog, ever closer to the inhuman voices, ever closer to the shoals, where the outgoing tide met the incoming wind and waves in terrible battle. The waves, as we were forced into shallow water, drew closer together and steepened. A little before sunset I could see the captain general gesturing first to our bow, then to the nearest shore, then I guessed he was planning to run the ships aground. But a wave mightier than the rest came crashing like an avalanche into our stern. There was a sickening crunch, an even more sickening lurch, and the main ship broached to. Our rudder had been torn away, and I watched in horror as the first mate, a man I had sailed with for over five years under my dear departed lord, was sliced in half, the bottom portion of his body shredded away with that rudder.

And then the fog finally caught up and swallowed us.

For perhaps a minute we drifted at the mercy of the waves and mist, unable to get our bearings or see our own hands in front of our faces. It finally dawned on me that we were doomed, but I underestimated the captain general's seamanship. He shouted orders, and our crew began to lower the mainsail and hoist a jib. Slowly and painfully the main ship came up into the wind. We were now less than a hundred yards now from the estuary's sandbar, but by skillful use of our sail we were able to crab sideways, making for the spot where, in comparatively sheltered water, the sandbar abutted the shore.

There was a rush for the bow, much screaming, much shouting, and Mephisto of all people grabbed my arm. 'The captain general is dead.'

'What?' I couldn't believe my ears.

'He's gone. The boatswain came for the tentacles in the steward's quarters, and his soul. You're in charge now.'

'But I—I—' A part of me was confused; speechless, too, for lack of a better word. This chaos was happening so fast.

'The moment we touch, you must jump,' Mephisto urged me. 'But watch the waves, lest they suck you back.'

'What about you? Where are you going?'

Mephisto pulled out his giant axe. 'To kill the boatswain.'

As I took my place at the rail with the remaining mutineers, it looked impossible for anyone to survive in such a maelstrom. The fog that surrounded us only made things worse. But a second before we struck, the jib was flung over. The ship spun about and, as she grounded, the bulk of her hull protected us for a moment from the oncoming waves. Something made me turn around. I froze briefly. For a moment I saw a dark silhouette standing portside with eight tentacles scanning its surroundings as if they had a life of their own. The figure was holding Mephisto's axe in one hand, a fish hook in the other. A muscular body lay dead at his feet. I presumed this to be the dreaded taskmaster, who had spent many a day taunting me when I was chiseling at ice in prisoner's leggings.

There was a cry of 'Jump!' and all around me men were leaping overboard, then scrambling up the sandbar to safety.

Not a moment too soon, I launched myself over the side. Even as I landed, with a thud that knocked the breath out of my body, the ship swung clear and a great wave came surging toward me across the beach.

What little remained of the armada was swallowed up by the fog. Truth be told, I was lucky to still be in one piece, find dry land when I did. Oh, and have my head still sitting *upright* atop my shoulders.

What few of us remained were marooned, proof of the wrath of the boatswain and his gloomy hell beside him neck in neck, let loose this very night. Thankfully, that befouled darkness was no longer approaching. Soaking wet, we had only our knives and the clothes we stood up in, and already the sand was veneered with frost. As luck would have it, however, the end of the bar was covered with scrub, which we cut into a great pile of firewood. With flint and steel, I managed to strike a sufficient spark to set it alight, and soon we had a great pyramid of flame which bathed the estuary in light. It gave off enough heat that we could scarce approach to within twenty paces. Dawn found us rested, dry and tolerably warm.

But most of all...alive.

'We must head inland,' I pointed to the mountains that ran parallel to this new foreign shore. 'Survival awaits us there.'

There was a general murmur of assent.

There is, I think, small point in further chronicling all that we saw and suffered during our arduous voyage. A diary consists of many hundred sheets of parchment on which to write, day by day, record a description of the people and places we visited. To fathom the unfathomable. To explain the unexplainable. It is a rare document, and often two or three extracts from it will conjure up, more vividly than words of wisdom, both the wonder and the misery of one man's voyage home.

And my companions I would remember even more vividly. Most of all, the boatswain and my master. It was strange, I thought, how I worshipped the ground both individuals trod. I suppose, like all of us, he was a complexity of good and bad. But one thing I am sure of. One day the boatswain will take every last seafarer in these straits to the stars.

And when man has voyaged beyond the farthest star, yet will there be one place still uncharted, one last corner of hell whose cosmic and cult-like mystery remains inviolate.

The seaman's heart.

# THE END OF ALL TIDES

## Paulene Turner

Pirate Captain Dustin Crowe regarded himself in the looking glass and liked what he saw. His newly-washed hair bounced with each sway of his ship, the Mermaid's Breath. His face was clean and close-shaven. He wore new breeches, black boots and a tailored beige coat with two dozen pearl buttons.

'What do you think?' he said.

From behind, Charly, the cabin boy regarded his reflection. 'You look like a fine gentleman, Captain. It's amazing how a well-cut coat can conceal a lifetime of sins.'

'Not a lifetime,' said Crowe. 'I had a few years when I was too small to do much mischief. But I intend to make up for the lost years in those remaining to me.'

'Well, if they see through your disguise tonight, sir,' said Charly, brushing fluff from the captain's shoulders, 'you won't have many of those. You'll be swinging in a pirate cage while crows feast upon your eyeballs.'

Far from being alarmed at the prospect, the pirate captain seemed amused. His cheek dimpled and his eyes shone like beetles in the lamplight. The chance of treasure with a side serve of danger always had that effect, Charly knew.

By daring to do what others dared not, Captain Crowe had become—at the age of four and twenty at most, by Charly's estimate—one of the most successful pirates upon the sea.

Still, the cabin boy felt someone needed to be the voice of caution. 'Captain, have you considered tonight's event could be a trap? If I were you, I'd stay well clear of an exhibition called *Pirates: End of An Era*. It seems an obvious way to lure the few remaining free seafarers into the net.'

'Yes. Sounds like fun, doesn't it?' Crowe said. 'I hear there will be some items from the treasure of Captain Morales. If I could obtain one of those, my captaincy would be assured for a few more turns of the tide.'

'So, you're planning to *steal* the exhibits? And who is the current owner of said items.'

'Oh, you wouldn't know them,' Crowe mumbled into his shirtfront.

It took a deal more probing before the captain revealed that the exhibition was being hosted by the King's Navy, with one Captain Hastings Broadbent as Master of Ceremonies.

'Broadbent?' Charly was horrified. 'The pirate hunter? But, Captain, that's too risky, even for you.'

As he adjusted his lace cuffs and cravat, Crowe's playfulness ebbed briefly. 'With the tide turning against pirates, the time is coming when we'll all need to risk much to survive as free men upon the seas.'

'Well, I wish you luck, sir.' The cabin boy said. 'And hope all I've taught you of manners and the ways of gentlefolk is enough to ensure your safe return.'

'Ensure *our* safe return, Charly. You're coming with me.'

'What? I can't go.'

'If I'm to pose as a free man of means, I'll need a servant to attend me. Who better than you, who has served gentlemen before? If I say something out of place, or forget which fork be for fish and which for fowl, you can kick me. You should enjoy that.'

'But how will I fool anyone looking like this?' The boy's striped shirt was threadbare. His pantaloons resembled remnants of a shark's supper. 'Not even a shipmate with both eyes out and their brain half-eaten by crabs would mistake me for a gentleman's servant.'

The captain pointed to some new clothes on a chair at the side: breeches, white shirt, green tailored jacket. 'I had Miss Annabella whip them up for you.'

'But...how did you know my size?'

'I had your measure, young man, the moment I laid eyes upon you.'

He held the cabin boy's gaze that bit too long, making a tide of blood rush to Charly's cheeks. Was he aware that Charly was short for Charlotte? That the cabin boy was a girl in disguise, Charly wondered? A 17-year-old well-born young lady running from an unsuitable match made on Destiny Island—in whose hidden coves they were currently moored—her home, before she escaped to sea.

'Please Captain, I don't think I should go.'

'Get dressed. Dobbs will row us ashore.'

#

The moon was high as they crossed the black water. Crowe cut a fine figure in his new jacket, his handsome profile outlined by moonlight's ghostly pen.

Charly huffed and leaned back. Of two things she was certain. One, Dustin Crowe was reckless. Two, although he was a thief with a girl (and seamstress) in every port, he wasn't a bad man. And the way he hung on that rigging!

Crowe turned just then, caught her looking. And winked.

With her face burning hot as a ship's barbecue, Charly peered into the dark water, wishing the cool depths would open up and swallow her whole. A white streak swam across her vision.

'Something's down there.'

'The ghost serpents are active, tonight,' said Crowe.

'Ghost serpents? I've never heard of such things.'

'They say serpents only emerge when blood's about to be spilled,' said Dobbs, his voice like shells cracking under a boot.

'Long as it's not ours, ey, lads?' said Crowe.

#

After a fifteen-minute walk through the bush, the trio arrived at the port of Destiny Island. A dozen rough-hewn buildings lined a beach arcing around a harbour, where two navy ships stood at anchor. Along the bay's entrance, metal cages creaked in the breeze, skeletons and half-rotted corpses slumped inside. The air was a pot-pourri of dead fish, ale and vomit. Home sweet home.

The centre of the activity was The Siren's Song, a two-storey tavern, where a dozen men in blue and white naval uniform crowded the entry, clanging tankards and laughing. Across the road, Charly spied dark shapes on the beach, which she assumed were rocks. As they drew closer, she saw they were men, drunk and drooling, as pigs foraged in the sand around them.

'Before we go in,' Captain Crowe pulled Charly into the shadows of a palm tree, 'if I give myself away and the worst happens, you be sure to get back to the ship and set sail with the others.'

'I'll return to the ship and fetch the others so we may come to your aid.'

'No,' Crowe said. 'As your captain, I'm ordering you to look out for yourself in the event of strife. That's how we pirates operate.'

'But if we don't help each other, what chance will we have against the navy? Sticking together is the only way we'll win.'

Captain Crowe was unusually serious as he swept a strand of hair behind her ear. 'Sometimes one must be sacrificed for the good of all.'

Heading back along the beach, Charly almost trod on the hand of an unconscious man. It was whipped back just in time.

'Take care, Captain,' she whispered. 'There are some who appear the worse for drink but who may not be so.'

A second look at the tavern revealed sailors unsteady one minute, sharp-eyed the next. Crowe's raised eyebrows confirmed he'd seen it too—an army of guards positioned to block all escape.

Still, he grinned as he went inside.

#

'Oh, yes. This is most assuredly a trap,' Charly said.

More than fifty guests had squeezed into a small room on the tavern's upper floor. About half wore His Majesty's blue and whites. The rest sported a riot of colours and styles that screamed *pirate*.

There was Captain Ezekiel Dreadnought, in a pink satin shirt with a tangle of gold necklaces, slipping food from the buffet down his trousers when he thought no one was looking. Pock-faced Abril Curtis stomped about calling the king's sailors "bilge rats" and "lily-livered vermin". Lady Captain Marietta Lyonnaise with a cleavage you could lose a ship in, held her pinky aloft, feigning delicacy, while tearing into her food like a wild dog.

'This will be the easiest win Broadbent's ever had,' Charly said.

The exhibition items sat on a table at the side. There were treasure maps, compasses, a "captain's necklace" of severed thumbs, some foreign coins and shells. The main attraction was a tarnished gold bell in a glass case. Engraved on the bell's underside was *The Death Knell for pirates will be heard at the end of all tides.*

'The bell's over two hundred years old,' Crowe whispered. 'We've all heard of it. According to legend, it will toll out the last free pirate upon the seas. The inscription is carved into every pirate's soul.'

'But what is—' Charly hushed until a blue-and-white had passed. 'What is *the end of all tides?*'

'It could be that moment when the tide turns, water flowing neither one way nor the other,' said the captain. 'Or a point on the map where currents disregard the rules of the sea. It's not clear. What is certain though is there's not a man here tonight who doesn't want to claim that bell and send it to the depths, ne'er to be seen or heard of again.'

Charly noticed clusters of colourful guests whispering around the case.

'They wouldn't try to steal it, here, would they?'

But of course they did. It began with footsteps upon the roof. A hole appeared in the ceiling, a fishing line dangled through wiggling its way towards the bell case. The only thing on the hook in the end, though, was the would-be thief, taken to the port jail to await Gallows Friday.

A second pirate tried sawing through the floor, hoping to pluck the prize from beneath and slip away before anyone noticed. However, his calculations were off and he sliced through a naval officer's big toe instead.

Captain Curtis preferred a direct approach, swinging a rum bottle at the case. A blue-coated arm shot out and caught it just in time and him with it.

'Fire!' someone cried, but no one so much as turned around; it was such an obvious ploy to clear the room and purloin the prize.

'The salt must have corroded their brains,' Charly said, shaking her head. Captain Crowe chuckled, but there was glint in his eye not put there through drink which made her suspect he had his own scheme for securing the bell.

'Stand aside!'

The crowd parted and a man clutching a large jar pushed through the guests. In his mid-years, with tight curls and eyes the colour of fish scales, he wore a well-cut maroon coat that impressed even Crowe.

'A late addition to the exhibits!' he announced, dropping the jar heavily upon the table. Inside, floating in liquid, was the head of an old man with one empty eye socket, mouth agape, as if in surprise, and long, grey hair that moved like seaweed.

'Friend of yours?' Charly asked, as she felt her supper trying to make a comeback.

'Captain Albert Greybeard,' said Crowe. 'One of the more successful pirates upon the seas. Until recently, evidently.'

'Welcome to the end of the pirate era!' the man in maroon bellowed. 'I'm Captain Hastings Broadbent, curator of tonight's exhibition and the King's chief pirate hunter. Some of you may have heard of me.'

'Blaggard!' someone called. As the blue-and-whites wormed through the crowd seeking the speaker, Broadbent slowly beamed.

'On display tonight are artefacts from an almost extinct breed— the pirate,' he said. 'They're commonplace now, but one day they may be worth something. Even Greybeard's head.'

His officers were the only ones who laughed.

'But that's not why you're here,' he said. 'The siren's song which drew you tonight are the treasures of Captain Morales. Among them, shells which reputedly whisper to sea creatures, coins that lead the way to safety. And the bell, the famous *Death Knell* for pirates.'

Charly watched Crowe as he listened to Broadbent. He wore a half-smile but the mirth didn't reach his eyes. There was an intensity there, a cold, still focus she'd only ever seen on him in dangerous situations at sea. It made her wonder whether the pirate and the naval captain had sailed in the same turbulent waters at some point in their careers.

'Is the Morales legend true?' Broadbent eyed the rapt crowd. 'Could an old bell end the pirate menace? My first instinct was to say: Rubbish! But now, I'm a believer. Because this exhibition has been the death knell for all of you.'

The pirates looked around, baffled by how anyone had seen

through their disguises.

'You've had a good run!' Broadbent continued. 'But it's over now. Your time is DONE!'

At his nod, the navy swooped. After so much food and rum, the pirates were easy to apprehend. Especially as they'd left their weapons at the entry door.

An officer pointed a sword at Crowe.

'I'm not a pirate!' said the captain, pushing the blade aside, as if it were distasteful to him. 'Do I look like one of them?'

The officer scratched his head, unsure. Until, from the side of the room, a older, well-dressed man, with a wine-barrel belly hastened forward. 'We vouchsafe for him,' the man bellowed. 'He's a friend of the family.'

Charly was surprised to see the speaker was the Governor of Destiny Island himself—her father. Turning away quickly so he wouldn't recognise her, she could barely fathom what was going on here. How do the two men know each other? Could it be a coincidence?

As the officer moved off, she heard her father whisper to Crowe: 'Our deal?'

'Where's the real bell?' said the pirate.

'Your man has it below. And your end of the bargain? Where's my daughter?'

Time seemed slow, like a wave rising and swelling before it crashed upon the shore, as Crowe turned her way. 'There she be.'

The Governor's eyes filled with tears at seeing his daughter again, but Charly couldn't shift her gaze from the captain's face, as she struggled to comprehend his betrayal.

'We need this bell,' Crowe murmured. 'It was the only way I could secure it.' At least he had the grace to look guilty.

Head lowered, the pirate captain headed for the exit. Halfway to the door, someone stepped in to block his path. 'Do we know each other?' said Captain Broadbent. 'I never forget a face.'

'I'm sure I'd remember meeting the famous pirate hunter,' said Crowe, smiling-not-smiling. 'Tell me, is it true what they say? To catch a devil, you have to be as bad as—or worse than—the devil yourself?'

Steely gaze met iron glare, neither giving way until...

'Hastings! It's me, Charlotte! I'm back. I've had the worst eight months imaginable! Come! Let me tell you about it?'

'Charlotte? Dear God!'

As Broadbent moved to greet her, Captain Crowe slipped out behind him.

Charly smiled warmly at the officer, giving her best performance of the night.

#

She was sixteen, and pretty. Captain Broadbent, in his late thirties, seemed old to her. But her father encouraged the match and the captain was so attentive and charming, she thought she might learn to love him. Until, one day, she saw him scolding a sailor for a minor offense. When she teased him about being grumpy and suggested he give the man a second chance, Broadbent smiled with lightless eyes. 'Why don't you focus on pretty dresses, my dear, and leave crew discipline to me.'

Later, she overheard him advising a newly-married officer to keep his wife "good and pregnant" so she wouldn't be tempted "to meddle in the affairs of men ".

The next day she ran.

#

Crowe found Dobbs on the beach, with the Morales bell in a sack. By moonlight, he inspected the engraving and confirmed it was the true Death Knell. Before setting off, he glanced back and saw Charlotte in the tavern doorway, her expression strained with disappointment.

But he'd had no choice.

Crowe had met the Governor during his week ashore and heard the story of their missing daughter, Charlotte. Bit by bit, he'd pieced it together. A glimpse at her sister's cameo with Charly's profile upon it confirmed his suspicions.

He wanted the Death Knell. They wanted Charly. A trade seemed in order. Crowe guessed that Broadbent would never put the real bell on show with so many pirates about. It was not too difficult for the

Governor to discover the location of the true treasure and, with Dobbs' assistance, secure it.

'Stop!' said Crowe, as he and the pirate were halfway back to the ship. 'I've made a mistake.'

#

'Crowd that canvas and be quick about it!' Captain Broadbent commanded his crew on the Regency. 'We chase the Mermaid's Breath.'

More than a dozen men shot up the rigging and along the yards to unfurl the sails. On deck, a line of men hauled rope as the ship headed towards the dark horizon.

Tonight was shaping up to be an historic night, Broadbent considered. Thanks to his brilliant plan, most of the pirate menace was now under lock and key on Destiny Island, awaiting Gallows Friday. Using the Morales treasure as a lure, he hadn't needed a single cannon to net the entire fleet of scoundrels.

Well, almost the entire fleet. One pirate by the name of Dustin Crowe remained at large. Though, with Charlotte's insights on the location of the Mermaid's Breath and her old captain's preferred sailing routes—obtained during her time as a hostage on that vessel—Broadbent was confident Crowe would be the next fish wriggling on his hook.

Broadbent scanned the ocean. As sea spray caressed his face, he licked his lips. Victory was close now, so close he could almost taste it—salty, like the pirate tears that would flow when Crowe and his crew were imprisoned with the others.

Once he'd achieved that and had rid the seas of all pirate kind forever, the Admiralty would look to him in awe. No longer would they pass him over for promotion or laugh behind their hands at him. They would make him one of their own.

*Admiral Broadbent.*

He liked the sound of that.

'Captain,' the helmsman cried, arms bulging as he struggled with the ship's wheel. 'Something's caught on the rudder. Something big.'

The first mate peered over the side. 'There's seaweed around the boat. White and thick. I've never seen its like.'

Broadbent squinted through his looking glass along the black horizon. Still no sign of the pirate ship. 'I don't understand how they got so far ahead. Unless your daughter lied, Governor, about the direction the ship was headed.'

'Why would she do that?' said the Governor, beside him. 'Pirates stole her from her home and those she loved. They're no friends to her.'

Maybe it was true, and maybe not. Perhaps she'd turned pirate after being crimped by them—it wouldn't be the first time such a turnabout had occurred. She could be feeding him lies now to send him off course and ensure they went free. If so, he would not be merciful. The only thing he hated more than pirates was a woman who took him for a fool.

'You up top, Harris! Can ye see any ships! Report!' Broadbent shouted.

A speck high on the mast descended, becoming a blob, then human-shaped until Captain Dustin Crowe dropped gracefully to the deck.

'Harris is tied up at the moment,' he said. 'But I can tell you there's nothing much out there. Only fish and whales and ghosts of crewmates thrown overboard.'

'You!' said Broadbent. 'How did you get here? Where's your ship?'

'Don't need a ship. I caught the wind and flew across.' Crowe made wiggly hand gestures.

When a sailor gasped, Broadbent whipped around. 'Only way he could fly is if I shot him out of a cannon, which I might yet do. He must have stowed away.'

Pistols clicked, swords zinged, all pointed at Crowe. 'Steady, gents. I'm here to negotiate with the captain.' The pirate reared back, palms up in surrender.

'I do know you,' said Broadbent. 'You were on my crew before we were taken by those pirates.'

'Aye, I was on your crew,' said Crowe. 'You stole me, from my bed, in the middle of the night when I was thirteen. My friend, Isaiah, the cabin boy, was a year older than me, when you found dirt beneath his fingernails at dinner service and threw him overboard.'

38

'Isaiah? Hmmm?' he shook his head. 'Sorry, don't recall the name. There've been a lot of dirty cabin boys during my career.'

At his signal, two hefty men flanked Crowe, grabbing an arm each and dragging him to the side. They hoisted him onto the railing so his legs dangled over the water, grasped his shoulders, ready to push.

'That bell you had on show was counterfeit, wasn't it?' Crowe cried out.

'How do you know that?' Broadbent demanded. 'Have you—?'

'—seen it, nicked it, hidden it. Push me over now and it will be lost forever. Along with your chance to gong us out of existence, Mr Pirate Hunter.'

#

Broadbent's cabin was crammed with charts, navigation instruments and keepsakes, including a mini-gallows with pirate in the noose carved from black stone. Captain Crowe played with it as he bargained with Broadbent.

'I'll give you your bell. On one condition,' Crowe said.

'What's that?'

'I get my cabin boy back.'

'And why would you trade a valuable treasure for a cabin boy?'

'I'd just got him trained up. Makes him a treasure to me.'

There was a knock and a woman entered. She had long golden hair, and a blue dress, cinched at the waist, highlighting her sea blue eyes.

'Evening, Madam,' said Crowe, then looked again. 'Charly, is that you? You mean you're a...blonde?'

'Hastings, don't believe anything this man says,' said Charly, her accent refined. 'He's an inveterate liar and thief who uses his friends to get what he wants.'

Crowe flinched at that.

'Whatever you did for him in that cabin must have been extraordinary, my dear,' Broadbent said. 'He came here today to trade his future and that of his fellow pirates for your company.'

'I did no service for him, but what a cabin boy does for a captain.'

'No one laid a finger upon her,' said Crowe. 'We didn't even know she was a girl.'

'Come on! Not even pirates are that stupid.' Broadbent leaned closer to Crowe. 'But I promise whatever it was you so enjoyed with her, I'll be doing it five times as often, and twice as well.'

'You are no gentleman, sir!' Crowe recoiled.

Charly slapped the pirate across the face. 'What would you know about gentlemen? Filthy pirate!'

As Crowe rubbed his pink cheek, Broadbent snorted. 'Laying it on a bit thick, aren't you?' he whispered to Charly. 'Not that I didn't enjoy the show.'

'I don't know what you mean,' she said. 'I remained loyal to you, Hastings, in every way. How may I prove it?'

Before he could reply, a sailor burst in. 'Captain, we've found the Death Knell.'

#

Crowe was lashed to the mast. As the moon broke free from the clouds, it spotlighted a golden bell hanging from a rope on the yards.

The crew stood quietly by, their usual bluster muted. Charly was up front with her father, the Governor, as Captain Broadbent paced the upper deck, in a gloating mood.

'Thanks to your woeful attempt to hide the bell, we find ourselves here, at the end of the night, at the end of the life of pirate Captain Dustin Crowe,' he said. 'And, with so many pirates dead or awaiting the gallows, it's not overstating it to say this is the end of the line for pirates. For too long, they've plagued our seas. Tonight we'll be rid of them once and for all.'

'Hear, hear!' said the officers.

Captain Crowe sniffed loudly, as if a tad bored.

'So, Captain Broadbent,' said the Governor, 'will you be ringing the Death Knell, to toll the end of an era?'

Broadbent sighed. 'I'm sorry to have to tell you but it's just an ordinary bell. I've rung it many times. Mornings and evenings, right on the change of tide, when not a drop of water stirred. And nothing happened. It seems the Morales myth is just that. A story.'

The ship jolted suddenly, throwing everyone off balance.

'Captain, we're stuck fast,' said the Helmsman.

'How can we be stuck in the middle of the sea?'

Fifty pairs of eyes peered over the side to see the black water turned white.

'White eels are all around the ship,' said the first mate.

'Ghost serpents,' whispered Charly.

'It's the Morales curse!' someone called. 'We're doomed.'

'Next fool who says anything like that goes over the side.' Broadbent's eyes swept the crew.

'Captain,' said the first mate. 'We're moving neither forwards, nor back. Remember the inscription: The Death Knell for pirates will be heard *at the end of all tides*. What if this is it? The end of all tides? Then now would be the time to strike.'

With a smirk at Crowe, Broadbent slowly moved over to stand beneath the Death Knell. He reached up and grasped the rope. But he didn't pull. At that moment, his gaze fell upon the water, thick with white eels, and he thought he saw green eyes peering back at him.

'Captain?' the first mate said. 'Is something wrong?'

Broadbent eyed the bell with suspicion, then let go of the rope. 'I don't think we need to bother with that superstitious nonsense.'

'Very wise, Captain,' called Crowe. 'Cause if you did, you'd be ringing yourself out of existence too. You're a pirate hunter. What use is that if there be no more pirates upon the sea?'

'Shut it, Crowe!'

'Once we're all gone, do you think you'll be promoted, get invites to the Admiralty club?' Crowe shook his head. 'Those blighters don't see you as one of their own, else they wouldn't have left you out here, salty and sun-scorched still chasing cut-throats and one-eyed thieves after all these years.'

Broadbent knocked a crew member aside in his haste to reach the pirate. He yanked Crowe's head back, drew his knife and pressed it to his throat. 'Say goodbye to all things worldly, Crowe.'

'Wait!' Charly moved through the men to Captain Broadbent and whispered in his ear. 'If you still care for me, you'll take Crowe back to the jail to face His Majesty's justice. Then I will not have to live forever with an image of my husband gutting a man.'

The captain's hand shook with his desire to plunge the knife in and wipe that sneer off the pirate's face. However, hearing Charlotte refer to him as her "husband" had excited him more than he cared to admit. As had the brush of her lips upon his earlobe.

41

'How do I know you're not protecting him?' he said.

'Him? Please! I only feigned friendship with him to preserve my life,'—Charly looked to Crowe—'though I loathed every moment in his presence.'

The pirate's grin faltered then, Broadbent noted, as he re-sheathed his knife. 'Very well. I'll enjoy watching you kick your last, pirate.'

A mist rolled in, as light and lithe as water sprites. More than one sailor muttered it was "unnatural". Broadbent went to chasten them, but the words froze in his throat as he thought he saw a cloud rearrange itself into the face of a man.

'Broadbent!' The Governor noticed pearls of sweat on the captain's brow.

'If you ring the bell and nothing ungodly happens, the men's senses may be restored. And clearly, Crowe doesn't wish you to ring it, which is reason enough to do it, in my opinion.'

Broadbent glanced back at the mist. The face was gone. It was but simple fog now, as, doubtless, it always had been.

'Very well.' He smoothed his jacket, gathering his self-composure, then looked up at the bell. 'Would you please chime the bell, sir?' He turned to the first mate.

'Me. But sir, I—' The man's eyeballs were moons atop his cheeks as he regarded the instrument. 'Morales was a pirate. They're tricky blighters. What if a curse falls upon the one that rings it?'

Crowe began chuckling.

'Quiet!' Broadbent called. 'The bell is named the Death Knell for pirates! Ergo, it's bad for them. Not for us. If anyone will be cursed, it will be Mr Crowe himself.'

'Captain Crowe,' the pirate corrected him.

Broadbent ignored him as he went on. 'There's nothing to be afraid of. Now ring the damned thing!'

The first mate reached up but his arm froze halfway. Crowe's cackling grew louder.

'SHUT! UP!' Broadbent gripped his knife handle so tightly his knuckles blanched.

'I'll do it!' Charlotte's touch on his arm was reassuring. 'You were concerned I might be protecting Crowe,' she whispered. 'Let me ring the bell and show you where my loyalty lies.'

*The Death Knell...for Pirates will be heard at the end of all Tides.* Charlotte read aloud the words inscribed on the bell's underside. Though she spoke softly, her voice carried across the sea.

'Farewell, pirate captain.' She looked over at Crowe. And winked. Then pulled the rope.

The Death Knell rang clear and strong, a wave of sound that seemed to ripple through the mist. The crew watched cod-eyed, grouper-jawed as the ragged wisps of cloud reshaped themselves into human forms. Ghosts of pirates with tricorn hats, tattered clothes and eye patches strode across the sea as if it was solid earth beneath their feet.

Charly dashed over to Crowe and slashed his ropes. Together, they watched as fifty or more ghost pirates reached the ship then continued right through the hull onto the deck. Men fell to their knees, weeping, pleading for mercy.

'Grimsby, is that you?' Crowe spoke to a ghost with two holes in his torso. 'You look...good.' The spectre tipped his hat to the captain and went to join a group of ghosts surrounding the first mate.

'Get back!' the officer screamed, slashing at his attackers. His sword sliced through the empty air. The ghosts jeered and advanced upon him. The officer moved back and back again, till he felt the rail behind him.

'Boo!' Grimsby whispered. Scared beyond reason, the first mate jumped over the side, landing with a splat rather than a splash on a thick weave of serpents. He tried to stand but slipped and fell. A serpent slithered over his torso. Another covered his upper body and legs. They dragged him down with a slap, slurp, squelch that made the bile catch in sailors' throats.

'They're going after the officers,' Crowe whispered. 'Broadbent's men, who did wrong by them whilst they were among the living.'

Ghost pirates formed a knot around six more officers. Three jumped overboard. One was blown over by a spectral wind. Broadbent's living crew threw one particularly hated superior off the ship.

The last officer clung to the side, waving his pistol to keep the living at bay. Behind him in the sea rose a slimy white head with two lurid green eyes. The serpent wrapped itself around his neck and hauled him backwards.

No one spoke. Or moved. For moments, stretched by terror, the only sound was the creak of ship's rope.

On silent feet, the ghosts assembled beneath the upper deck, as if awaiting the captain's address. They began to sing, a haunting Yo Ho, Yo Ho, a Pirate's Life for Me. A scrawny boy ghost broke from the crowd, climbing the stairs to where Captain Broadbent cowered.

'Isaiah,' Captain Crowe whispered to Charly.

The boy's ghostly brow furrowed, as he scraped at his fingernails with a spectral knife. Then presented his hands to Broadbent for inspection.

'Is that better, Captain?'

Broadbent nodded and the boy beamed, with real delight.

Now, the ghosts advanced on Broadbent, climbing the stairs, cursing him and blowing wind so hard his way, the captain's skin was taut as canvas in full sail. Still, he clung to the rail. 'Get back! I'm captain of this vessel! You can all go to the devil!'

Behind him, a monster arose from below, composed of many sea serpents entwined. It kept rising till it was almost as tall as the mainmast. The captain cried out in terror as he saw dozens of unblinking eyes focused upon him. The creature opened its mouths and moved in for the kill.

'Wait! Crowe's voice came from behind. 'Allow me!'

As Broadbent turned, the pirate's fist slammed into his face. 'That's for Isaiah.'

Broadbent staggered back and over the railing. Splat, he landed. Squelch, slurp. The serpents sucked him under.

Isaiah bowed to Crowe. And the ghosts turned to mist which blew away in the breeze.

Only then did the bell stop chiming.

'Look lively, lads,' Captain Crowe called. 'We've had enough sea for one night. Make for land.'

'Aye aye, Captain!' they shouted with feeling.

So, Dustin Crowe commanded the Regency back to Destiny Island. All aboard had agreed to join his pirate crew.

'Seems like pirates will be around a while longer, then?' Charly said.

44

'Be a bit boring otherwise,' said Crowe. 'The King's officers would have no one but cabin boys and deckhands to pick on. And we couldn't have that, could we, Charly boy.'

Crowe grinned and leaned on the railing beside her. Together, they watched the moon's reflection riding the liquorice waves.

'How long have you known I was a girl?' she asked.

'Hmmm. From the moment I first laid eyes upon you.'

Charly huffed and shook her head. He was smug and infuriating, but he had come to her rescue.

'Did you know the bell would work in our favour?' Charly asked.

'Did you?'

'When I saw the engraving, and that space between the words, I knew we'd been reading it wrong. It wasn't the *Death Knell for pirates*. It was *The Death Knell*—space—*For pirates shall be heard at the end of all tides*.'

'Smart lad. Sorry, lass.'

Charly tilted her head at Crowe, a vertical crease forming between her brows. 'You didn't come back here to save me, did you?'

'Course I did.'

'When you saw the inscription on the real bell, you knew it would save the pirates, not destroy them. That's why you stowed away and hid it so badly. You wanted Broadbent to find it and ring it. It wasn't me you came back for at all, was it?'

Crowe inhaled the fish-and-wet-wood scented air. Perfume to the pirate nose. 'There's more than one belle worth dying for.'

Charly looked out at the water, oddly, assuaged.

'Do you think Morales knew how clever he was putting that space in the sentence? My governess always said punctuation was important.'

Crowe grinned, moonlight catching his gold earring. 'What's punctuation?'

# *POLL PIRATE*

## Michael Fountain

From The Confessions of Poll Flanders: Being an Account of the Robberies and Murders of the Most Notorious Pirates, as told by One Poll Flanders, Who Sailed with Lawless Men, Buccaneers, Freebooters, Privateers, and Cutpurses, and Lived to One Hundred and Twenty Years of Age. Along with Digressions on Scurvy, the Pox, Loose Tongues, and the Horrors of a Lee Shore. For Such Moral Uplift as May Save Young Persons from a Sorry End, and Much Good May It Do Them.

I.

I was still in baby fluff and before me first molt when me old Da would say, 'There are three sides to every story: yours and mine and the truth.' Who's a "pirate", and who a "privateer", hoity-toity, with a government license to rob and murder, and which of us an honest parrot, trying to live free in a wicked world?

Most of my comrades having long gone by way of the step and the string, or drowned off Hatteras, or more likely drowned in a cup of sack, I am free to disclose the truth of a life spent on the account.

They call me Poll, or Polly, or Devil-Take-Ye as fond nicknames. Here I lay a primary feather aside my nose to remind the wiser amongst you that 'tis best not to give your True Name, as it may come back to hang you. One never knows when an honest bird might have to fly under a false flag to save his own skin.

The first name I signed on with was Poll Flanders, in honor of a Great Lady me Da was fond of, she who visited our rooms when I was a nestling, and fed me outen her own fingers, with fried apple pastie, and cream and rose water trifle. She were a great lady, so she were, and no bother to us if she hid certain treasures, informally acquired, under ouren nest, with instructions for us to shout nonsense and nip at such fingers as made rude inquiry, as to where she might have found such shiny things as might be reported missing by the gentry.

It seems humans do covet shiny things as if they were ravens and magpies. You cannot eat gold—no, I tell a lie. You can, indeed, eat gold, but it comes out the same as it went in. I have swallowed such nuggets as might do me good for my crop and my gizzard. But no one saluted me, or called me wise, or more beautiful, for having more-or-less gold in me tummy than any other bird.

So, with more gold in my stomach than money in my purse, Grim Necessity drove me to piracy, when I might have been a policeman or solicitor, and stole my money honestly.

Sure, as it says in Scripture, let them as is without sin cast the first stone. The point of which, is that if everyone be honest, no stone will ever be thrown, for we are all as steeped in calumny as the First Parrot, who was cast out of Eden for peaching on Adam and Eve, when he hollered 'Parrot wants some apple, too!' at the worst possible moment.

#

On Grub Street, the pamphlet writers posit a Golden Age of Piracy, from 1650 to 1730 or thereabouts. But pirates been pirating long as people been mucking about in boats, so that date's as random as you might throw a dart at an elephant then run and hope for the best.

Many a tavern brawl has old Poll started, saying, 'This here Golden Age starts when the Queen let loose the Sea Dogs in 1560, not 1650, and it ends when they hanged Charles Vane in 1721,' and already your timeline is tangled like a mare's nest. 'For Poll,' says I, 'the youthful joy went out of pirating on an April midnight, 1717, when Black Sam Bellamy went down off Cape Cod with five tons of treasure and 144 souls.'

Then another says, 'Villain, you lie, it's 1714 to 1722 if it's a day,' and another, '1726, or your mother's a rump-fed ronyon,' and now elderly professors are throwing fists like they should've done when they was twenty. Let's just call it end of the Sixteens and first half of the Seventeens, when pirates was pirates and ships was nervous.

Us didn't appear outen nowhere, like them soldiers who sprang from the ground when Cadmus sowed the dragon's teeth. They was a peely-wally king of Spain what died, and the other kings gave us license to attack another king's ships, then marooned us on the beach with no way to scratch a living.


II.


They was a sickly king of Spain, *El Hechizado*—Charles the Hexed, Charles the Witched, Charles the Cursed—who was taking his time a-dying. Mind, folks been waiting for him to die since the day he was born. They called him Cursed 'cause the poor devil had everything wrong with him you can imagine, and even some you can't. Sufferings of Job, as it were.

His jaw was too big for his face and wouldn't let him chew his food proper. On account of bad diet, his legs was so bowed with the rickets he couldn't walk 'til he was four. When he was dead for sure, and they opened him up to look inside, he had water on his brain, stone in his kidneys, and a heart the size of a peppercorn.

This might be on account of being as inbred as any old pharaoh. Them Habsburgs—Charles the Cursed was a Habsburg—was always marrying each other, to hold on to their property and keep the family business in the family. Egyptian royals married each other on account they thought the pharaoh was a god, and a god had to marry another god, but them Habsburgs did it for real estate.

If you's to draw up pedigrees, you'd see at least eight in-breedings in Charlie's family tree, all of which multiply his odds of inheriting them royal diseases. So, the king of Spain *was* cursed, not by witches, but by all the Habsburgs that came before him. Married twice without leaving any children on either side of the blanket, and now royals all over Europe is having fits over who will inherit the Spanish empire when he goes belly up.

Charlie wants his Spanish half to go to one of them Bourbons, a grandson of the king of France. King of France says; 'Oh, you must.'

The Habsburg relatives in Austria say; 'No, you shan't.' Then these little sea-going countries like Britain and the Netherlands say; 'No, you mustn't.'

No sooner is Charles the Cursed dead in the ground than this here War of Spanish Succession is on. Ten thousand dead here, twenty thousand there, kings and princes sending men to kill or mutilate men they've never met, over places they've never heard of, for rewards they'll never see.

You and I wouldn't give a fig or a fart, if it weren't for what the kings call a *letter of marque*, which is to say a license to pirate. This says you can do what you like, so long as you attack some *other* king's ships, and give your betters a percentage of the loot. With a letter of marque, you're not a pi-rate but a privateer—*corsair* as they say in France—and welcome in fancy salons.

Tis a way for the king to raise a navy on the cheap. A declared war is expensive in blood and treasure, but a privateer pays for his own ship, takes a prize, keeps a portion, and pays a percentage to whoever granted him license. An English privateer could attack a Spanish ship, but not an English or a Dutch, because the Dutchmen is our friends, this week anyways. And on some islands you were welcome as a dinner bell, but on others you'd be hanged without trial.

And if that privateer is caught and condemned, the king or queen can say, 'Who? Me? Francis Drake? Harry Morgan? Never heard of the scurvy fellows. You say they burnt your ships and took your gold? How dreadful! You has my deepest symphonies.' This here is what we call a legal friction, and I seldom saw a king who could wind his bottom or wipe his watch without some legal friction to excuse his naughty ways.

High Court of the Admiralty issues 1,622 letters of marque during the War of Spanish Succession. But the war ends May 7th and the Admiralty says as of May 8th, you can't be a pirate no more, or we'll hang you.

Figure each of them sixteen-hundred captains has a crew of twelve rough and ready hands, more like thirty or more. Sixteen hundred letters of marque times thirty, there's forty-eight thousand Englishmen cast ashore in 1714, never mind them of a Dutch or a French persuasion. Toss in the odd Spaniard, and Nigerian, and

Congolese, for a third of them was African fellas escaped from the Portugee.

There's Ben Hornigold, and Black Sam Bellamy, and Charles Vane, and the rest marooned with nothing to show. Us parrots can only count to six, but that's a lot of men fallen to hard times and penury. No pension from the Crown, no pay for lost limbs or missing eyes, no way to make a living except to raise the black flag. It was thus that grim necessity did prompt yours truly to wickedness, and I became an enemy of mankind, a *hostis humani generis* as the learned say.


III.


'Oh, but Poll,' I hear you say, 'you might still amend your wickedness, and give up piracy for a life of penance and good works.' And I might could give you a nip to teach you manners, but Poll knows it's the way of squeakers and fledglings to judge others and know what folks should do, better than they know what to do with themselves. Come back to lecture after you've made your own mistakes, and sermonize me then.

My learned friend Dr. Johnson—who I knowed from the river front where he walked to fetch oysters for his cats, Lilly and Hodge, on account he didn't want his household to resent caring for them— Dr. Johnson says, 'No man will be a sailor who has contrivance enough to get himself into a jail, Sir; for being in a ship is being in a jail, with the chance of being drowned. A man in a jail, Sir, has more room, better food, and commonly better company.'

Complain and you catch it for sassing your betters. The captain of the Rochester whipped a young sailor to death with a tarred rope an inch thick, six hundred lashes he whipped him, first screaming, then keening, and it took a horrible long time for that boy to die. Would make a parrot wish his eyes tore out, seeing how they done. Bill Richardson told me he saw a sailor flogged to death for losing an oar over the side. And that were a slave ship, with worse practiced on the souls trapped below.

Look here, an honest sailor in the king's navy, avoiding all sin, got paid out two pounds a month for bad food, bad water, a cruel captain with the power of life or death, away from home for years at a time, and the chance of drowning for someone else's mistake.

Find honest work ashore, you say? On land they was two hundred and twenty crimes punishable by death. One of them French coves said the law treats everyone equal, because both rich and poor are forbidden to steal bread or sleep under bridges.

I've seen what Man does to Man for want of potatoes and butter and bread. Tis true, a bird needn't think about poverty, as like the lilies of the field I toil not, neither do I spin. Yet Solomon in all his glory and his three hundred porcupines is not arrayed in such finery and feathers as the Lord provides such as I.

'In honest service,' Bartholomew Roberts said to me, 'there is thin commons, low wages, and hard labor. In this life on account (by which he meant pirating), there's plenty and satiety, pleasure and ease, liberty and power. And who would not balance their credit on the side of piracy, when all the hazard that is run for it, at worst, is only a sour look or two at choking? No, a short life and a merry one shall be my motto.

Lived to thirty-nine he did, kilt by grapeshot, and his body dropped overboard dressed in his finest clothes, afore the Andrews could get they hands on it. Or so they say, as they never found his body, and I would not be surprised by word that Roberts is signing on new hands, and I bless us all with his favorite toast: *Damn to him who ever lived to wear a Halter!*

IV.

How fat were they, them fat Spanish ships as we waited to pounce upon? Them Arawak folk as Columbus landed on had no gold of their own—Devil take him, he cut off their hands and sold their children to make them give him their gold when they hadn't aught but a few trinkets. And once the *conquistadors* found the shiny stuff amongst the Aztec and the Inca—Well, now the fox was loose among the chickens.

I can give you one raid alone, that Poll knows more about than he should, when Drake attacked the mule train carrying Inca silver from Peru to Nombre de Dios in Panama. We, I mean Drake and the cimarrons, took 25 tons of gold and silver off them mules. Reckon 32,000 ounces in a ton, times 25 is 800,000 ounces, near fourteen million British pounds in silver alone, not counting the gold. And that off one mule train.

Sure, didn't I get out my slate, and my friend Mr. Halley, to do the ciphering for me? Was off the coast of Africa, where he went to catalogue the southern stars. A gentleman fresh out of college, on his first great voyage, and he relished the chance to talk pirate-talk with old Poll.

'Poll,' says he, 'reckon 100 tons of gold and 25,000 tons of silver from Mexico and Peru, and the Spanish king got a fifth of that, and soon old Phillip will rival Croesus—' (him what invented money in the first place) 'To say nothing of the gold them conquistadors stuffed in their own pockets. You can bet they's creative bookkeeping going on, the king being five thousand miles away, and none the wiser.'

Mr. Halley, you can trust his figures. Why look here, didn't he reckon that the comet what appeared in 1066—when Willum the Conqueror and his friend Norman surprised King Harold Godwinson—was the same hairy star as appeared in 1682, and Mr. Halley's numbers said would be back again in seventy-five years?

Do I digress? Sure, that's where you find the real treasure, like when you're grooming for mites and find a fat juicy one.


V.


On paper at least, them Spaniards owned half the world, on account that a year after Columbus crashed into the Bahamas, the Pope drawed a line on a globe, and he give everything west of that line to Spain, and east of that line to Portugal. On paper that the Spanish owned North and South America, and everything in it, from Florida, south to the Argentine, and west to the Philippines. The Portuguee owned High Brazil, and west Africa, and east to India, and Macau in China, and Nagasaki in Japan. Never mind there was people already living there.

Aztec and Inca, silver and gold, and emeralds too. To carry all that from Peru to Spain, sail round the tip of South America—dangerous enough, with the williwaw winds coming down off the mountains, and gusts from behind every rock, and the oceans crashing together. Which is why on their first trip 'round the Horn, we baptize young squeakers with a bucket from the Pacific and a bucket from the Atlantic, if they ain't half-drowned and cold and wet enough already. Eight hundred ships lost there, and tens of thousands souls drowned, 'til the treasure that went to the bottom of the sea was more than was ever taken by pirates.

You might could sail into the Pacific instead and take the long way 'round. A hundred days without landfall, mad for want of fresh water, chewing boots and belts for somepin to eat, if the scurvy don't get you first. Should you reach the Philippines, it's another year or more to get home, assuming you don't die along the way like Magellan hisself, who volunteered for a war betwixt the Filipinos. 'The Filipinos be upon us!!' I cried, but too late for Ferdinand, as he were kilt by a poison arrow.

I again digress, but that's oft where the best bits are, like when old Poll bites his toenails and finds a goody.

You might load the mule trains to carry the loot from Mexico and Peru to the ships at Veracruz, or Cartagena in Columbia, or Portobello in Panama. But now there's nothing for it but to sail through the Caribbean, and thence to Spain.

That's why those under the black flag wait in the Caribbean. They's islands, and inlets, and coves at the mouths of rivers for pirates to hide and jump out at a fat treasure ship. Lonesome beaches to careen your ship if she needs repairs.

And Port Royal as a place to spend your money, for it don't do you no good to carry treasure around if you can't eat it, drink it, or wear it. The onliest time I knew pirates to bury a prize was when we took that silver train at Nombre de Dios—twenty-five tons, too much to carry away in one go.

But money and real estate are topics for old men. What you want is talk of mad kings and queens, and explosions and the lopping off of heads.

## VI.

I were but a squeaker and in my first grown feathers when I signed with Francis Drake and the Sea Dogs. That were the twenty-eighth year of the reign of Elizabeth, Good Queen Bess, or Liz-Bett as she bade me call her. That were the year we singed the beard of the king of Spain.

Now I see in the back a gentleman who attended the college of Well Actually. 'Well, Actually,' says he, 'Drake was a privateer and not a pirate.'

You mean that Francis Drake who plundered ships and cities on the Spanish Main, who sailed 'round the Horn to raid the towns on the Pacific coast, 'til his ship near sank from the weight of silver and gold? Who sank thirty ships at Cadiz? Who accused his shipmate Thomas Doughty of witchcraft, mutiny, and treason, so's Drake wouldn't have to share, then served a last meal and cut off Doughty's head? Drake, who first learned his trade on Jack Hawkin's slave ships? Privateer, forsooth!

T'would make a cat laugh to see the antics they got up to under cover of law. I would be honest about our dishonesty. If ever I am admitted again to the fancy tables of the Great, it will be due to my restraint, not hooting with laughter when a pirate calls hisself a privateer. And Elizabeth, Lord love Her, took half of what Drake stole, with little risk except to her reputation in Spain.


## VII.

Well you might ask how your old shipmate Poll found himself entangled with the affairs of the mighty. When we arrived back home, the Queen came out to the ship herself to knight Captain Drake, and collect her percentage of the loot.

And the Spanish king were none too happy, calling us pirates, having forgot that he pirated the gold from the Indigines. And so eight years later, he sent the Spanish Armada came sailing for to capture or kill our own Queen Elizabeth.

This particular war had its seeds back when Elizabeth's own Da was a sprat. They say he were a right charmer in youthful days, 'til he landed on his head in a tournament. Henry Eight was what we called Elizabeth's dad, on account his pa was Henry Seven.

You ask how I could know so much, but birds will talk, from your songbirds in gilded cage, to them ravens that croak around the Tower, and thus I repeat the things that were said and done in the chambers of the great.

When Eight was eleven, and his brother fifteen, their pa had papers drawn up to marry Eleven to a seventeen-year-old Princess of Spain, *hight* Catherine of Aragon. But Prince Eleven was most contrary, and he died afore the marriage could be complete. They say it was the sweats that kilt him.

'*El príncipe está muerto!*' says Catherine of Aragon.

'Poke him with a stick,' says Henry Seven. 'No one's going to cheat *me* out of five million in dowry, and an alliance with Spain.' And he turns to Henry Eight. 'You know wait this means, don't you boy?'

'No school tomorrow?' says Henry Eight.

'You're bound to marry your sister-in-law,' says Da.

'*Ai, Dios Mio!*' say Eight and Aragon together.

#

What about the war with Spain? Which I'm getting to, ain't I? It can't be all boy's adventure and explosions in this here tale. You think Drake sailed around the world in a straight line, and never a side trip for fresh water or citrus?

So Eight and Aragon was married for twenty-three years and set to brooding. Most all their hatchlings died, but for one they called Bloody Mary, on account she was hollering 'Off with his head! Off with his head!'

As I told her at the time, 'We can't cut all of their heads off, my dear, or the place would look like a bowling alley.'

'Off with *some* of their heads!' she said. 'Off with *some* of their heads!' Mary being always willing to compromise.

Now when Bloody Mary was herself fifteen, Eight declares that he will divorce Mary's mother Catherine. But the Pope in Rome said you mustn't, so Henry says to his lawyer, 'You tell the Pope that he grants me a divorce, or I will take my church and go home.'

'But why?' says Henry's lawyer.

'I have no son!' says Henry. Them royals was most particular that boy children be preferred over girls. 'And Catherine, she's not fun, she's not exciting, she's not—'

'She's not me!' says Lady Anne Boleyn.

'I'm not comfortable with this,' says the lawyer.

Now a king can be cruel as any pirate, and Henry made the lawyer ten inches shorter by lopping off his head. That head was parboiled and stuck on a pole, that they put up on London Bridge for all to see. I heard this from the raven who et his eyes, before the lawyer's daughter climbed up there to fetch it.

So long as he's picking a fight, Henry reckons the church has a lot of money tied up in real estate. So he closes the convents and the monasteries, kicks the monks and the nuns to the curb, and takes everything that wasn't nailed down. Eight starts his own church, patent pending, with himself in charge, and now the king can preen, sing, and regurgitate with whom-some-ever he wants, such being the way of courtly love for both peoples and parrot, that last to prove yourself a good provider.

Eight had his own selfish reasons, but the church itself was a right old mess on account of all that money laying around, and a pile of money attracts attention from the worst sorts of people. A family named Borgia was in control of the church in Rome, and it were a scandal to the jaybirds.

Them as protested against the Borgias they called Protest-ants. And some wanted to kick out the Borgias, they called your Reform-ation. Three hundred years after that of killing each other over whether Jesus had blue or brown eyes. You say tis but trivia, these wars of religion, but there ain't nothing so trivial but that humans will murder for scraps.

Anne Boleyn's daughter was our own Queen Bess, Elizabeth, or Liz-Bett as I calls her by her leave. Anne was pregnant twice more, but alas they miscarried, and the bloom was off the rose. Having discarded one queen, thinks Henry, why not another?

'Who's *that*?' says Henry.

'Henry Eight, Jane Seymour.'

And Jane Seymour says, 'Perhaps Your Majesty would like to— see more?' Her son became king at the age of nine, but by fifteen dead of shame, on account of that joke of his mother's.

Henry Eight sets his cap for Jane Seymour and gets rid of Anne by accusing her of treason and worse, and they lops off her head with a sword, Princess Elizabeth then but a child of three. Married three times more Henry did, 'til he transformed from dashing king to a bloated toad. 'One, two, three,' he says, 'four, five, six.'

'Are you counting your wives?' says the last queen, Catherine Parr.

'No, toes! I can't see mah toes.'

'Put your gouty foot up on this pillow,' says Parr, 'and we'll see if we can find those piggies.' And thus Eight breathed his last as she were counting up his piggy sins.

Young Edward gets the crown but he were dead soon enough. Names his cousin Jane Grey as queen, but Jane is a nine-day-wonder afore her head is lopped off by his half-sister sister Bloody Mary. 'Because I'm bloody Bloody Mary, and I know what's best for everybody!' says she. 'Off with her head! Off with *their* heads! And off with—*gaak!*' And the wretch dies of cancer.

Now Elizabeth is made queen, and up sidles Bloody Mary's widower, King Phillip of Spain. 'Thith queen eeth daid,' says he.

'Long live me,' says Elizabeth.

'Your Maggie's Tea,' says Phillip, 'let me express the condolences of Es-Span-yeh (as he were wont to say) on the death of your sister.'

'My sister that was your wife,' says Elizabeth.

'About that—' says King Phillip. And with Bloody Mary barely cooled to room temperature, this king of Spain hints that he ought to be the one to marry Elizabeth.

Elizabeth scorned the fellow, preferring the company of piraticals such as Drake and Raleigh and your Humble Servant. Held suitors at arm's length for the rest of her life, and so kept the crown for herself.

You wonder I can recite what was said and what was done. Tis my phono-graphical memory. I hear the Puritans in the back complain, 'yon bird is just parroting.' Tis their slander, that us repeats what we hear without thinking it through. And haven't I heard many a courtier parrot the party line to win favor, thinking it'll put them in good with the aristos. Such like to rub elbows with rich people; they think it's going to rub off on them. Better an pirate than a jackal living off scraps, says I.

Meanwhile a Scottish cousin, another Mary, hatched a very great many plots to have Elizabeth killed, until Liz-Bett can ignore it no longer and has Scottish Mary's head lopped off. This gave the king of Spain his excuse to declare war on his sister-in-law Elizabeth and send your Spanish Armada against the Sea Dogs.


VIII.


Spanish Phillip sent 137 ships, two thousand cannon, ten thousand sailors, and nineteen thousand soldiers to sail up the Thames, arrest Queen Elizabeth, and put a Spanish king upon the throne. We ourselves had 100 ships close to hand, but only 40 of them were warships.

'Most of them wrecks is antiques, and good for naught but burning,' says I to Drake, which sparks a light in his able mind. Spain had the ships and the guns and the armies, but Elizabeth had the Sea Dogs, and her spy master Walsingham.

It fell upon me to smuggle myself onto a Spanish ship and feed them bad advice. Which I was then disguised as a pious pet of the Spanish Inquisition, a parrot who spent long hours in prayer.

As I was praying, Drake and the Sea Dogs loaded eight of them old ships with powder and brimstone, and soaked rags in tar and pitch, and lit them on fire. And when the enemy were off Calais, the English set them eight little fire-ships to drift in amongst the Spanish Armada, slow to turn, made of wood and loaded with powder.

The Spaniards they seen the fire ships a-coming. 'Why ain't you praying, Cardinal Parrot,' they cried, me being dressed in red as part of my disguise.

'Got what I was praying for,' says I.

There was no time to haul anchor and get away from the fire. I told them to cut their anchor cables, and a wind blew us away from England and into the North Sea.

The Sea Dogs were blocking their retreat. 130 Spanish ships had no choice but to sail around the northwest of Scotland and try for home through the Irish Sea.

But now storms was blowing them towards the rocks of the Irish coast. And having cut loose their anchors on account of my bad advice, they had nothing to hold the ships off the rocks.

There I am, dressed in red like a cardinal, having convinced them to cut their anchor ropes in the first place, and about to be smashed on the Irish rocks. A Spartan at Thermopylae might have gone down with the ship, but I quick tallied how much them Spaniards owed me from dice the night before, and asked myself whether it was worth following eightpence to the bottom of the sea, and so I bid a fond farewell to such inhospitable climes.

Just then the Spanish commander, one Medina Sidonia, ordered that the horses and mules of the Armada be thrown overboard into the billows of the sea. Just as I would not drown myself, so I could not endure the screaming of them Spanish horses, and so picked at their main tether until I had it undone, and snip, snap, bit through the last of the thread; and then nip, nap at the flank of the eldest. And so started them charging for the rail, and them Spanish horses jumped off the burning ship into the billows of the sea.

I fear some was lost in that first plunge, God's Mercy on us, 'til the sea shall give up her dead. But one, then two, then several few horses came snorting up. And one bugled, smelling land I suppose, and they all started swimming for the shore.

I fluttered down to perch on the crest of one mare's neck. I then proceeded to the poll (aptly named) behind her ears, and from there called the rest to hearken to me.

'Pull, you dog's dinner!' I shouted, 'Swim for your lives! Swim, or I'll skin you myself and wear your hide to church! You crib biters! You wind suckers! Pull, for your mother's shame! Pull for shore!'

The Spanish horses formed a flotilla and made for the near shore, necks straining, legs paddling. They snorted, they trumpeted and whinnied to one another, but they swam. They had to!

We stumbled onto the shore at Connemara in Ireland. And on that boggy shore we met a few scrub ponies, once ridden by the blue-painted men who rode for kings of Ireland before even the Celts arrived.

Love was soon in bloom, and the Spanish horses with their Arab traits married the Irish horses with their own fierce ways, and thus the Connemara pony was born, and the ponies of the Shetland Isles, and the New Forest ponies in Hampshire. And never a word of their debt to old Poll, for introducing their grannies to their grandsires.

Tis said that such horses can see spirits, and if you look between their ears you might see 20,000 Spaniards waving from the bottom of the sea, dressed in strange costumes and speaking that strange tongue.

Near froze I was when I made it to Clare, hoping to sign with Grace O'Malley on the White Seahorse. But Liz-Bett's spymaster Walsingham was expecting me, and weren't I faster with a message than horse or ship? I flew to London in less than a week. A pigeon might have got there faster, six hundred, seven hundred miles in a day, but I am a sensitive soul who needs fruit for his tiffin, not your dry seeds and twigs that a pigeon can roost on. These big parrot brains won't feed themselves! And if I must stop at an inn for a roister, who's to say it weren't earned?

Walsingham already knew that the Spanish invasion had failed, on account that he weren't dead yet. Never no piece of the puzzle so small that Walsingham could not fit into the rest to make a picture, him being founder of the British secret service.

#

More I could say of Drake's sad end, when he sailed again for Panama to die of the dysentery, vomitus at one end and loose stool at the other. Or some history of pirating, in the antique days of Jewels Caesar, and the pirates he crucified, on account they had no taste for poetry. Of Henry Morgan, who sank two of his own ships through drunkenness. Or Anne Bonny, and Calico Jack, and Edward Teach, with his fourteen wives and fuses smoking in his beard.

But I should have to be in the Caribbean to meet those worthies, and in 1695, I had signed with Henry Avery, and did witness such things in the Arabian Sea as would harrow up thy young blood and turn you away from this pirate life.

IX.

There is a legend, and alas that's all it was—that one Henry Avery, or Every as some spells it, who set himself up as a pirate king. That he married to a sultan's daughter, that he rules over a city of 12,000 pirates on the island of Madagascar. That in 1694 he stole a ship, called it Fancy, and went to prey on the Hindoo and Musselman ships that sail the Indian Ocean and Arabian Sea, that he took a ship worth six-hundred thousand British pounds.

I do not tell of Henry Avery to entertain, but to brace you amidships, that for all the fables we conjure, at the edges of the map there are cruelties not to be spoke of. Not all pirates was friends of the common man, and mayhap this is where you learn some hard truths.

A bear or a tiger might kill you because they're hungry and you're an extra bit of provender, or they got a youngun nearby, or you surprised them at stool, but there's no malice in it.

Henry Avery was a hell-kite, a cycle-pathic killer as they calls them, on account they lurk near cycle paths to jump out at the unwary. But rest you easy. There be'nt as many cycle paths as you might think from your Jacobean theaters, where there's poison in every cup and a dagger up every sleeve. You watch enough of them theatricals, and you'll think there's a cycle-path around every corner. Old Poll's been at sea these many never-you-mind how many years and seen all matter of blood and entrails on the deck, but only met one true cycle-path, and that was Henry Avery.

This is why yours truly found religion and repented of my sins, not for hope of admission to Heaven, but because if I got to Hell I fear I would find not the Old Nick, instead there's Henry Avery sitting on the Serpent Throne, having snuck up behind the devil and slit his horrible throat. I'm saying I'd rather meet the Prince of Lies himself than be in the same room with Henry Avery.

#

On the London stage tis play-acted that Avery fancied himself a Robin Hood or Alek-Sander, and married a Mogul princess, and that his crew honorably married the Moslem ladies, with a Mussleman priest to officiate.

But in truth as I am told by birds of the Moha to Bombay trade, Avery's men tortured the crew in horrific ways, and forced themselves most horribly upon those ladies, and insulted them so that they threw themselves into the sea rather than live. Days of this while Avery dozed, and counted his gold, and permitted these crimes to his eternal infamy.

The Fancy escaped by sailing to Nassau, and shaking bags of gold under the governor's nose, said that every member of the crew would give the governor 20 pieces of eight and two pieces of gold, and Avery was to pay a double share.

Many a vicious pirate is forgiven his sins by waving money at the law. 'All the people see how Arabian gold works with some consciences,' it was said at the time.

And many an upright hypocrite is easily led to favor these enemies of mankind, when they have hopes of sharing in their criminal wealth.

Governor Nicholas Trotter of Nassau asked that each member of Avery's crew would give him 20 Spanish pieces of eight and two pieces of gold, and he would allow the crew to spend their money in Nassau. And their captain—Avery pretending to be a man named Bridgman—was to pay a double share.

The East India Company and the king's navy was watching for him in the Indian Ocean off Bombay and Calcutta, and the Arab sea west of east Africa, little knowing Avery was hiding in plain sight in Nassau. The Fancy, already rotting away, was beached on Hog Island, and Avery vanished softly and suddenly away.

#

When I were a sprat, money meant solid coin—none of this paper money claptrap. For me, if you had more gold and silver than you could carry, you went to a goldsmith and asked him to keep it in his safe. He gave you a written note, saying how much gold or silver you had in his vault, and you could take that to the shops. The merchants started trading the notes instead of the coins, to cash them in later. That was as close to paper money as I ever wanted to get.

The Bank of England had started handing out bits of paper to pay for another war with France. How was I to know that you could exchange them bank notes for honest coin, or pay for things with just a scrap of paper, if it was covered with the right signatures and shibboleths?

Now paper money can be et, though tis better for shredding into your nest, as I had occasion to on my first command, being let out in the captain's cabin and trusted around his paperwork. I thought the printed bank notes so pretty, with their printed emblems, and names of the banks who issued them, and a thing called a cheque, with writing on it, a kind of letter to draw cash money from the bank.

Such pretty, bright paper I could not resist, and tore off great strips for my nest, and Henry Avery saw what I had done, and Holy Church, how he did scream.

Now I was very proud of my nest and thought it should rival the finest lacemakers and pullers of tow, and preened a bit, which was my pride going before my fall, for that was the end of my naval career.

Avery said he would see me cashiered and strangled, and drummed before the fleet, and keelhauled, and boiled, and plucked naked without a feather or a farthing, and all such horrors in various order—for how should I be keelhauled, if I'd already been plucked and cooked and eaten? And if the great cabin had not been fitted with windows for my escape, it would have gone hard with me.

To be accused of theft in this affair of the shredded bank notes was no small offense. As we say in our pirate codes, 'If any man rob another, he shall have his nose and ears slit.' I'm not one to cast aspersions, as I may or may not have nipped a nose or an ear in a spirited moment, but where's the man's humanity? Some say dead in a ditch, some say he's gone to Madagascar.

Thus cast adrift, without friends, without feathers—for in his reckless haste, Captain Avery and his cutlass had trimmed my tail when he meant to spear me through—I turned to the popular press and an ink-stained amanuensis to relate my *General History of the Robberies and Murders of the Most Notorious Pyrates*, printed under the pseudonym of Captain Charles Johnson, it ben't no easy thing for an honest bird to collect royalties, with these liars and thieves up and down Grub and Fleet Street.


X.


Thus I freely give this account of my life among the pirates, in hope that telling the truth to shame the devil might slip me into Heaven, when Jack Ketch knocks at the door and it's Poll's turn to take that long walk on a short rope. But I may yet take to the account again and cheat the hangman.

As that squeaker Ben Franklin says—a squeaker, I say, him being but twelve years old the year Ned Teach's head was hung from a pole—*It's better to swim in the sea below / Than to swing in the air and feed the crow / Says jolly Ned Teach of Bristol*. That were the first broadside the printer Franklin hawked on the street: *A Sailor Song on the Taking of Teach or Blackbeard the Pirate*.

Not that I begrudge the crows a meal, but I hold close me old Da's lesson, that your Puritans prate their Ten Commandments—Thou Shalt Not This and Thou Shalt Do That—but they forget the Eleventh Commandment, which is Don't Get Caught, as it says in Scripture.


*NOTE.*

Here the narrative of Poll Flanders ends, as a messenger arrived, who whispered only: *A bonny lass, May Day, Charles Town, Noon by the clock*. Whereupon our feathered informant excused himself, saying he long suffered from catarrh and the lumbago; and after the company left by the door, it must be presumed he flew by the window, for he never was seen more. Having claimed to have witnessed three generations of pirates, presumed drowned, or taken by a cat. Never swung on the gallows, nor peached on his fellows. Writ here 1730, in the third year of the reign of his Majesty George II, long may his reign drag on.


*AMENDENT TO THE EDITION OF 1730.*

It has long been held that this account of Poll Flander's disappearance from the historical record took place as described, his end as mysterious as the final whereabouts of Anne Bonny after 1721, or the cryptogram left by the pirate La Buse when he hanged in 1730.

Around the corner from Dr. Johnson's house in London is a four-hundred-year-old pub, the Cheshire Cheese. The building at 145 Fleet Street has held a tavern since 1590, and indeed, the Cheshire was the first public house to reopen after the Great Fire of 1666. Fleet Street then being famous for its newspapers and printing plants, the Cheshire Cheese swarmed with journalists and other ink-stained wretches wandered up from Grub Street. Dickens himself warmed his feet by the fire after his twenty-mile walks.

There may you find the stuffed remains of an elderly parrot referred to by the tavern's familiars as Poll. When asked if the bird were related to the historic Poll Flanders of pirate narratives, who disappeared the same year La Buse was hanged, the bird affected coyness.

At its height the British Empire contained more than three hundred languages. Add to that the thousand languages spoken across Africa, a thousand more from Native America, the 400 indigenous languages on the Indian continent, and the several Celtic languages still found in the British Isles.

A reporter arriving in London from distant lands was eager to get to Ye Olde Cheshire Cheese, first for a ginger beer and then to teach Poll Parrot some new profanity from the far corners of the world.

Thus Poll might call Lord Beaverbrook a "vile ranting Tory dog" in Yoruba, Chug, or Proto-Bantu. He was said to be fond of using Sanskrit to address any visiting royals, calling it the "language of the gods" when expressing his terminal disgust with aristocracy. The clicks and pops of the Khoisan tongues were reserved for distaff members of the press such as Nelly Bly; Poll was a great groomer of feminine hair and biter of ears.

On Armistice Day, 1918, Cheshire Cheese Poll imitated the popping of a champagne cork 400 times, and dropped from exhaustion. This was the first sign of advancing age. The bird survived until at least 1926, when Poll's death was reported by the BBC as "International Expert on Profanity Dies".

The oldest parrot in scientific record lived to be 83 years and 58 days. It strains credulity that a bird who knew Blackbeard in 1716 might have escaped justice until 1926. Nevertheless, we ought not underestimate the ruthlessness of a bird sworn to life on the account, who might well fake his own death to escape the noose.

Until such time as testing can be applied to the taxidermized individual at the Cheshire Cheese, we cannot assign a definitive end to the career of Poll Flanders, still listed among the missing, loyal to the pirate credo of a short life but a merry one.

# THE GHOST

## S. B. Watson

'Her name ith Charity.'

Hamlin slouched against the frame of his chair like a sagging skeleton, his crimson justaucorp hanging open, revealing the soiled cotton shirt beneath. One arm draped across the battered wooden table where papers lay fouled in a vast spillage of rum that glistened beneath the swaying light of the overhead ship's lamp. His head rolled on his neck as he spoke, his forked tongue flickering between ancient, crusty lips.

Captain Hamlin was drunk.

'Thay hello to me mate, bitch.' Reaching out, he patted Charity's head, ran blackened fingernails through her faded gold curls.

Charity said nothing, only stared forward, unmoved at the man's wizened touch.

Hamlin laughed, the split tongue clawing through his ratty beard.

'Charity doesn't say much, these days.' When he switched to French, the lisp disappeared.

The door to the captain's cabin shut behind me. The crew had decided—my course was set.

The flintlock slid from my coat. I poured the powder as he spoke, and rammed the ball down the barrel.

He babbled in English first, before wandering into broken Dutch. 'Count me thelf lucky, I do,' he hissed. 'Never alone, these last ten years. All the ships, all the seas, and men dead and drowned... But these last years, there's always been Charity.'

I pulled the hammer back.

'You remind me of thomeone,' Hamlin rasped suddenly, leaning forward and peering across the table, spreading the pool of spilled rum until it drooled over the edge to the floor. 'Another negro...

Y earth ago.' His voice had darkened.

My grip froze upon the pistol. Did he recognize me? How could he? It was a lifetime since we'd met; I was only a boy then. He couldn't. We'd already been at sea three months...could he hide it that long? Only revealing it now, here, deep in the bottle?

'Thit thy-thelf down,' he ordered, taking his fingers from Charity and pointing at the empty seat across from him.

The cloth of my shirt stuck to my chest beneath my coat, clammy and moist in the damp heat of the cabin. Sweat broke across my forehead.

'Sit,' he commanded again, in French.

Under his trance, I stepped slowly forward, boots shuffling through the broken bottles and torn charts littering the deck. I pulled out the chair across from the captain, but did not sit down.

'She was beautiful, once,' he said, quietly.

For a moment, beneath the sallow light of the overhead lamp, we both remembered.

#

'You purchase these for your master?' the voice asked, behind me.

I assumed the woman was talking to someone else, and kept close eye on the hunch-backed old trader, carefully shoveling hard-shell nuts from the small barrel on his counter onto the scale. He paused to glance up at me from beneath overgrown eyebrows.

'Boy,' the voice snapped, suddenly close.

I spun around on my heel, head lowered, and clasped my hands behind my back.

The woman stood before me. With my head down I could only see the narrow toes of her boots peeking from beneath the dusty hem of her petticoat.

'Do you understand me?' she asked, in sloppy Portuguese. 'Look at me.'

I looked up.

'So, you do understand me...'

She was tall, and thin, with sharp eyes set above drawn, fair cheeks. Whisps of flowing golden hair escaped the drooping bun that sagged at the back of her head, and trailed across her sun-freckled neck. She wore a long-sleeved, jacketed bodice of dark green, open in the front to expose the swell of her freckled chest. Her skirts were the same green material, dark, embroidered with golden fronds. It was clearly expensive, yet the collar was frayed, and the depth of the fabric faded and grown shallow.

The woman herself was faded, in fact. Lines etched her glinting eyes and creased the corners of her mouth.

'Those nuts,' she said, leaning down to look me straight in the face. 'They're for your master.'

I nodded.

'What is his name?' she asked.

There was something in her voice that made me hesitate.

Without blinking, her arm whipped out, cuffing me against the side of my head, sending me sprawling back into the trader's counter.

'What is his name?' she hissed.

'Hamlin,' I gasped from the floor.

The woman straightened, her gaze already wandered from the little black slave crumpled at her feet.

'Tres, Dois,' she called. Two blacks appeared from the shadows, lumbering like tigers. 'Come,' she said, and with a rustle of skirts turned and swept to the open door, disappearing into the humid afternoon.

The slaves followed; the one called Dois grinned at me as he left. His eyes were yellow and his teeth were orange. The door slapped behind them.

'Take the nuts and get out,' the trader snarled from behind the counter.

I pulled myself up from the dirt-smeared plank floor, paid the man with the money Master had given me, and rushed out the door.

Outside, the oppressive heat fell upon me like a moist blanket. Overcast skies hung over the drooping palm trees that dotted the street, bristling in the sickly African heat between the old, white-painted buildings of Bandy. In the distance, ship masts prickled above the red brick roofs from their mooring in the Rio Real—the slavers, bringing goods to the local Ibani warlords in exchange for blacks, like me, from up north.

The woman and her men were nowhere to be seen.

From the master's great bay windows, the old mangrove swamp seemed to stretch away forever. Shafts of evening sunlight broke through the gnarled old trees, swatches of fuzzy light hovering across the dark, still waters.

I stood near the door, very still, the way Slang had taught me, my feet together, head lowered, hands clasped behind my back. Slang paced slowly before the bay windows as he spoke. In the afternoon glimmer, the master sat at the long dining table, listening, quietly shelling nuts.

'You say she had gold hair?' Slang barked. He was a big man with skin a shade lighter than mine, wide jawbone, and strange, curled tattoos tracing the contours of his face. He wore simple breeches and a loose cotton shirt, covered by a jerkin.

'Yes, sir,' I said.

'A white.'

'Yes.'

'Portuguese?'

I stammered. 'I don't know.'

'Dutch? French?'

'I don't know.'

'But she had slaves?'

'Yes,' I said.

'And she knew the captain's name?'

From the long dining table, the master spoke before I could answer. 'English,' he said, in the same tongue. He'd poured the nuts into a wide silver platter on the table, and held a large walnut between his fingers. 'She is English.'

'It might not be her,' Slang said, standing still before the shifting evening light of the swamp.

'It is,' said Hamlin, placing the nut on a small leather tray and selecting the proper tool from a little kit that never left his table. Today, he used the pointed compass... At least, that's what it looked like—it had two metal arms, sharpened to points at one end and hinged with a turnscrew at the other. 'She's come,' he said, his accent gentle and musical as he struck the pointed arms down into the nut.

70

Slowly, he turned the screw, forcing the two arms apart. The shell crackled, and split.

#

Slang returned from town late that night. The servant's quarters had been an old storeroom; Hamlin repurposed it for his house staff when he bought the plantation. From my bunk I could hear their voices in the dining room, low and laced with venom.

'I waited three hours...' Slang said, trailing into a language I'd never heard before.

From a low murmur, Hamlin responded. '...as long as you were meant to wait. Yet it's no matter. You spoke with the king?'

My breath caught in my throat.

The murmured voices trailed away again, leaving only whispers.

'The price doesn't matter,' Hamlin said, his voice rising. 'They have no concept of my wealth. They are war pigs, led by the fattest feeding trough. All they need is silver, and...'

The voices died down. A moment later I heard a door close. Footsteps approached the servant's quarters. I rolled over, curling up in the thin cotton sheet, and rammed my eyes closed.

Slang opened the door and stumbled in, the reek of rum and spirits wafting from him. He clamored in the dark to the empty bunk across from mine, where he occasionally slept when working at the main house. Strange words escaped his lips, sounding like evil incantations. I heard his body slam against the hard cot, his breath panting the damp air. My own breath I held, willing myself to become invisible.

Slang had nightmares. He would whimper in his sleep. Growl and moan. When he awoke, he would sit on the edge of his bunk and recite strange prayers, peppered with Dutch and French oaths. Tonight, his breathing fell silent in minutes. I listened to the hoarse rise and fall, the stink of his body reaching me across the room.

'They're ghosts,' he told me once, hissing through his chipped teeth. 'Ghosts of all the people I've killed. They've been set free, you see...to torture me.'

#

It was late when I awoke, dragged from my bed by the heels, the thin sheets snarling around my shoulders and face. My head hit the floor still wrapped in the sheets. The wind was knocked from my lungs.

At first, I thought I was dreaming, but the kick in my side hurt too much for a dream. I heard the snapping of ribs and a searing pain leapt into my chest. I scrambled up, trying to escape the sheets, stumbled over something, and fell again, the sheets slipping from my face.

A shadow stood over me in the darkness, illuminated by the weak light from the open door behind him. The shadow grinned, and I saw orange teeth.

Dois grabbed me by the collar of my shirt, wrapping his knotted fist in its fabric, and dragged me from the servant's quarters into the dining room.

The lamps were lit. The room hung in a sickly yellow pallor. A night-time chill had fallen, and a poor fire guttered in the old fireplace in the great wall. The master never used it—swore the chimney was clogged. Smoke curled from the fireplace into the room, filling the damp air with a dusty haze. Outside, the mangrove swamps reflected red in the night... Too bright to be a reflection of only the dining room. Flickering red.

The plantation was burning.

Dois dragged me across the room. Pain from my rib flared in my head as I tried to gather my feet beneath me. I only saw the figures in the room dimly, standing like specters in the smoke. Dois threw me into the corner with the other house slave, a small boy from the kitchens.

'That's all from the house,' Dois growled in French.

The figures swayed in the smoke. I curled on the floor, gripping my side in pain. As Dois stalked away, I surveyed the room, my grimacing face pressed into the floor.

Hamlin sat, bound to a high-backed chair, his wrists tied below his armpits to the frame so his fingers stuck forward like little clipped wings. His legs were tied at the knees and ankles. His head had been strapped back with a belt. Slang lay on the floor next to him, hog-tied into a ball and gagged. Hamlin wasn't gagged, but said nothing nonetheless.

Through the room stalked the big lumbering slaves I'd seen the day before, plus others, hulking men in soiled breeches and loose cotton shirts. One stood by the far door. One stood at the window, peering out. Another crouched by the fire, poking at the flames, seemingly impervious to the smoke creeping from the plugged chimney. Dois stood by the door to the kitchens. Nobody spoke.

Slang strained against the ropes that tied him. They creaked under the man's great strength, but didn't slip.

Hamlin sighed, the haze shifting around him. 'Give it up, Slang,' he said, in Dutch. 'No mortal man could break those ropes.'

Dois looked up angrily. 'What did you say?' he snarled, stepping towards Hamlin. 'You speak French, dog, or don't speak at all.'

In French, Hamlin said 'I called your sister a whore.'

With a grunt, Dois sprang forward and buried his fist into Hamlin's stomach. The smoke swirled as the chair toppled over. Dois began savagely kicking the master. Beneath the blows I could hear Hamlin rasping for breath. Slang struggled against his bonds again, to no avail.

'Enough!' The sharp voice of the woman cut through the air.

Dois froze. All eyes turned to the door from the kitchens.

The woman from town stood before it, with Tres and the largest man I'd ever seen, a towering slave, so tall he had to lean beneath the jamb of the door. As she spoke, the giant and Tres slunk into the room.

Tonight, she was dressed like no woman. She wore old soiled trousers and boots with a loose cotton shirt, unbuttoned partway down her chest, revealing the sway of her bosom as she moved. Her hair was coiffed behind her head. In the smoke it was hard to see, but dirt or blood seemed to be smeared across her left arm. Short calfskin gloves covered her hands.

'Pick him up,' she said.

Dois scrambled to heft the chair upright. Hamlin started to laugh, guffawing when Dois dropped him in his haste. 'Gently, boy,' he hissed. 'I'm sure your sister'd be ashamed of your lack of grace.'

Even through the smoke I could see the veins rippling across Dois' forehead as he tried to control himself. He dropped the chair upright, lurching Hamlin against the ropes.

'Now back off,' the woman commanded, and walked towards the master.

73

'Why, bless me soul,' Hamlin cackled in English, 'it's the good Mrs. Adolf Esmit. What brings you to share in me hospitality, Charity?'

'I'm surprised you even dare to think Adolf's name,' she said, stopping in front of Hamlin, and leaning down to look closely at him. 'You're older,' she said. 'Not so dashing as you were then.'

'You too, hag,' Hamlin said.

Charity didn't rise to the offense. She responded softly. 'Yes, I'm afraid the years in St. Thomas' dungeons, with my husband, took what beauty I had left.'

'I heard you came back for him,' Hamlin said. 'Stupid of you.'

'And what if I loved him?'

'Even stupider.'

The giant kicked out the guttering fire in a blaze of sparks and smoke.

'Why are you here?' Hamlin asked, in French.

Charity straightened to her full height and glanced at the table.

'How did you find me?' Hamlin tried again, in English.

'Took me years,' Charity said, moving to the table and picking up a walnut from Hamlin's platter. 'But eventually the rumors of the great Jean Hamlin led me here, to Bandy, where I saw a little black boy, buying nuts, just like good old Jean used to prefer.' She turned to look at Hamlin. 'Adolf died in debtor's prison, in Courland.'

'As a man soweth...'

Charity picked up the pointed compass, and turned it under the lamplight. 'Where is the silver, Jean?' she asked.

'That's why you've come?'

'Twenty-four thousand pounds of silver we hauled in that night, under the cover of darkness, before Le Trompeau was torched in the harbor at St. Thomas. Twenty-four thousand pounds of silver the governor—dear Adolf, my husband—helped you save before your ship was destroyed. Helped you transport overland. Helped you load into The African Merchant.'

Charity turned in the smoke, pointing at Hamlin with the compass. 'Twenty-four thousand pounds of silver Adolf never saw again, along with the pirate who stole it.'

Hamlin laughed.

'My dear, my dear... That silver is in the bottom of the bay, with

74

the bones of Le Trompeau. I'm surprised at you, swallowing that old legend.'

'I helped unload it myself, under the guns of Fort Christian,' said Charity.

The venom was so intense in her voice Hamlin paused.

'Very well,' he said, the mocking lilt gone from his words. 'It's here,' he said. 'This house. This plantation. It bought it all. The land. The slaves. The silver... It's gone, woman. Long gone.'

A smile creased Charity's lips. 'I thought you might resist,' she said.

Hamlin frowned beneath the belt banding his forehead. 'It's the truth, girl.'

'As a man sows, so shall he reap,' she said. 'We have all night, before your plantation burns, Jean. You were known for your tortures. See, here...' without turning she swept her hand across the table behind her. 'You even kept your old tools. Repurposed for cracking nuts.'

'The silver is gone,' Hamlin snapped, beginning to strain himself against his bonds.

'We have all night,' Charity said, again, moving into Hamlin. The glint of scissors flashed in her hand, rising to the master's face. Hamlin clamped his jaw shut.

Charity laughed and reached back to the table.

'Just like old times, then,' she said, grabbing the strange, sharpened compass. 'The *Speculum Oris*, or am I mistaken? Your favorite tool for opening closed jaws, sitting just here, among the nuts...'

She thrust the pointed tips through Hamlin's lips, leaning against the man, the chair straining under her backwards pressure. Still holding the scissors in her right hand, she turned the screw. Hamlin's mouth opened wide, snared against the iron arms of the infernal device. Fearless of Hamlin's bite, Charity reached into his mouth, yanking his tongue out with the grip from her gloves.

'This is for all the things you could have said, to save my husband,' Charity whispered, hoarsely, as the scissor blades tightened length-wise upon Hamlin's tongue.

Hamlin's breath grew sharp, panting a panicked rhythm. The scissors closed in Charity's grip. Hamlin roared. Blood bubbled from his opened mouth, drooling down Charity's arm.

Laughing, she leaned back, one hand still holding a whipping strip of tongue from the cocked-open mouth. Hamlin's roar subsided, it appeared by a great effort, replaced by a guttering growl, fouled with blood.

'It suits you,' she said, wiping the scissors on his smattered jacket lapel.

Reaching up she yanked the *Speculum Oris* from his mouth, scattering tooth chips across the floor. Hamlin clamped his mouth shut immediately, puckering his red lips. 'Thlave in hell, bitch!' he cawed, thick red spittle splattering her shirt and face.

Charity put her head back and laughed, shrill and hard above Hamlin's rasping.

By now I'd raised myself to my knees, next to the little kitchen boy, both of us watching the woman's brutality in horror. The movement outside the window only caught my attention at the last moment. Tres saw, and called out, but it was too late.

The window behind me shattered in a rain of glass as the rock burst through it, shards slicing through the room. Wind whistled. Dois fell back against the dining table, gripping the long arrow shaft that stuck from his chest. The giant was struck twice, once in the head, once in the shoulder, and fell back into the fireplace, crumpled like a sack of grain.

Two of Charity's slaves turned and bolted through the doors; screams echoed moments later from the hallways of Hamlin's house.

In the silence, four men, black as pools of ink, stepped through the shattered window, tall bows, long arrows knocked, preceding them. Thick raffia skirts girded their waists down to their knees; dark bands of ash-colored cloth wrapped their forearms. Each wore tight helmets of hardened, dried raffia, their necks covered in draped cloth gorgets, laced with golden thread and dark-red beads. From the shadowed hallways, more warriors appeared, like shadows creeping across evening walls, dart-shaped swords hung at their hips.

Charity's slaves backed together, near the dining table. There were only four left alive. Charity still stood, frozen in place, next to Hamlin.

Hamlin began to laugh. 'Kill them all,' he hissed, in Portuguese, 'but leave the woman.'

The warriors didn't hesitate. The wicked swords flashed in the smoky lamplight. Three of the brutes were cut down and hacked to pieces on the floor. The fourth broke free, leapt through the window, and bolted into the night. The archers by the window raised their bows and let heavy arrows whistle out into the flickering darkness.

'Untie me,' Hamlin ordered.

The bonds were cut. Hamlin crumpled from the chair, and fell to his knees. For a moment, he held his face in his hands, before gathering feeble strength and standing to his full height.

The color had drained from Charity's face. She stood, still holding the scissors, eyes fixed on Hamlin.

'You're a fool,' Hamlin said, in French, blood drooling from his mouth. 'You of all people should have expected this...' He grimaced with every word, his face twisting into a hateful mask. 'Did you forget my deal with your husband, all those years ago? He sheltered me. He protected me. Why? Because I made it profitable for him...'

Turning, Hamlin waved his hand around the room, gesturing at the ring of warriors bristling against the walls.

'Where did all that silver go, woman? Look around you! It's here! It bought my land, it bought my house, it bought my protection from King Perekule of the Ibani! And again, why?' He looked back, sneering into Charity's face. 'Because I fund his wars and I fund his slaving. I pay into his coffers. Adolf ran his course. He got careless. It was time to cut him loose.'

Charity swallowed. 'He was imprisoned for piracy,' she said, her voice had lost all its power. 'You should have helped...'

'He was imprisoned, let off, and given his governorship back, thanks to your scheming,' Hamlin snapped. 'Yet he was hated by all, lost it again, and was finally cut off by the king of Denmark.' Then, in English, the horrid lisp slathering his words, '...ath a man thoweth.'

Hamlin turned to the warriors. 'Take her away and have her.'

Charity didn't cry out. She didn't whimper as the warriors threw her to the ground, tying her wrists with the very cord she'd used to bind Hamlin, didn't shrink from the hands that tugged and struck and pulled her back to her feet. She fixed Hamlin in a deathly stare, her haunted eyes never leaving him.

'I curse you,' she said, as they led her to the doorway. 'I curse you.'

After they left, Hamlin sunk back into the chair and buried his face in his hands.

#

'You've made a mistake,' Slang's voice said.

I sat up against the servant's quarters door, my ear pressed against the uneven seal at the jamb, listening. They'd locked us in, me and the kitchen boy, after the Ibani warriors left.

There was a pause, then Slang spoke again. 'You heard what she said? She cursed you.'

'Been curthed before,' Hamlin's voice returned, low, and frequently halting.

'If they kill her, she will return, Jean,' Slang hissed. The table clattered, as though he'd hit it. 'She will return and never leave. Every waking moment you'll feel her, standing there, behind you. When you sleep at night, she'll haunt your dreams. You'll never be rid of her, if she dies like this.'

'What am I to do then? Thee burned half my plantation, thee killed everyone but you and the two worthleth boyth, and...'

'Why, Jean?' Slang moaned. 'Why did you have to goad her?'

Hamlin snarled, pain lacing his voice. 'If she meant to kill us outright,' he hissed in French, 'we'd all be dead. Leading her to waste time was our salvation. Damn the king's warriors... Took their leisure getting here.'

'You'll be cursed.'

'Then what do I do? The die's been cast.'

There was a long silence.

'You remember when I joined you?' Slang said. 'You got rid of them, then. Threw them into the fire... They've all returned, Jean. They're here with me, even now...'

Hamlin's voice dropped so low I could barely hear it through the door. 'You can do it? Yourself?'

'Aye, I can do it.'

#

The door swung open early the next morning, tumbling me across

78

the floor from where I'd fallen asleep, still eavesdropping. I scampered up, expecting a cuff on the ears, but Slang was preoccupied.

'Get to the wagon, boy,' he growled, taking the store-box from its place beside the fireplace and setting it upon the table. He threw back the old, battered lid and put two fist-sized pouches on the table, each rustling with the sounds of coins and manillas. Cool morning light broke across the mangroves, a warmed breeze gusting in through the broken window.

Hamlin sat, slouched back in his chair, eyes closed, a grimace locked on his face. He wasn't sleeping, but breathed heavily nonetheless. His neck beneath his chin was swollen to the size of a melon.

I stood, frozen at the door, watching Slang inventory the contents of the box, counting out the barbed manillas, the currency of the slave markets. His hands moved with a frantic energy. Sweat dripped from the ridge of his nose, even though the morning was still cool.

Suddenly Slang turned, haunted eyes locking on me. 'I said *get*,' he snarled, stepping in my direction.

I turned on my heels and bolted to the wagon.

#

They had her in a cage, down by the river.

Slang and the tall dark warriors stood beside the corroded bars, looking in at her as though she were a wild animal, haggling in Portuguese. I was too distracted by the spectacle to listen.

Charity had been stripped and put in the cage with five or six children taken as spoils from the tribes up the river. She sat, blazing white in the rising light of the morning sun, her knees drawn up to her chin. Dark bruises bloomed across the pasty skin of her back and sides. Her eyes stared forward, vacant. Something inside the woman had expired in the night—this wasn't the same creature that cut Hamlin's tongue and laughed in the bloody act.

Slang took out the sack of coins, and gave them to the king's men. The warriors poured them out, counting the pieces of eight and manillas. They nodded. The sack was taken.

Then the gate was opened, squealing on its hinges. Charity looked up, dull recognition on her face as Slang grabbed her by the hair and pulled her to her feet. She stumbled to the wagon, where he wrapped her in an old canvas sailcloth, and put her in the back.

Then I was put in the cage, and the door was closed.

I watched as the wagon slowly trundled back up the track through the king's slave warehouses and disappeared between the trunks of the palms.

#

I was loaded on a ship, bound for the Barbados markets. We never got there. The slaves rose up and killed every white aboard. We even threw the mate's dog into the cold bosom of the sea.

For ten years, I sailed under black flags. Tortuga, Port Royal, and Isla Vaca were home; the far slave coast of Africa was a forgotten memory... Until one day I stumbled upon Jean Hamlin at the docks of Matanzas, fitting a small frigate for a voyage of fortune, looking for a crew...

#

The ship gently swayed in the night-time currents of the bay.

After all these years, Hamlin's voice still held a lilting music in the French. 'Aye, she was beautiful,' he said, 'but beauty isn't everything.'

Reaching out, he took Charity's shrunken head by its long fair hair and lifted it from the table. The head spun slowly in the air, the gut-sewn eyes seeming to survey the room. Hamlin squinted as he brought the head up to his face, his forked tongue wetting his lips.

'Knew a man, once,' he said. 'Shipped with me from Rio de Janeiro. Indian, on the run from his people. Came from some magic river, deep inland. He wore a brace of these around his belt, he did, when we took him. Said they held the souls of his enemies. I threw them in the fire the night before we shipped and damned if he didn't howl for years that their ghosts came back to haunt him. He boiled her head in my kitchen. Took six days.'

He laughed and dropped the head to the table. It rolled into the rum, stopping up against a clump of half-shelled walnuts.

80

'She's *my* only ghost, mate,' Hamlin said. 'Or would be, if I didn't keep her safely tucked away, in here.' He patted the head and grinned up at me. 'Bought her for one negro boy. Got the better end of that deal, I did.'

I pulled the pistol up to his face and pulled the trigger. Powder and flame erupted into the narrow cabin. Hamlin's head whipped back, thick blood speckling the stern windows behind him. He sat tense for a moment as the blood flowed down his face, fouling his shirt; then his body relaxed, hanging limp against the chair.

'As a man sows,' I said to the dead Jean Hamlin.

And so the deed was done, and I was captain.

Slowly, I reached out and took Charity's shrunken head by the hair, and lifted it. It was lighter than I expected, the skin shrivelled and grey. I held it before my face. I could still see the beautiful features I remembered as a boy beneath the crust of death.

A chill fell upon me. What was this thing in my hand? An ill omen? A curse? Or a talisman. As I watched, it seemed Charity's puckered lips began to smile.

I threw my head back and laughed. Fear was for boys; I was a man. When I looked back down, her smile had vanished.

I hung her head from my belt, and turned to the cabin doors. Charity Esmit was *my* ghost now, and it was time we faced our crew.

# *AND THE SEA*

## Jack Wells

October 13th, 1717
Brigantine Lacuna
Atlantic Ocean
400~ miles north-west of England

*Fair winds from the east; ship managing a steady 11 knots; crew are in middling spirits.*

*We've been over a month at sea, making north by west with all possible haste, though I have not been made privy as to why. All the captain will tell us is that we are after the prize of prizes. Some unclaimed booty from a previous confrontation.*

*Unfortunately, we have been forced to defer our quest out of necessity. That damnable Royal Navy frigate, our constant shadow for over a fortnight, has finally caught up with us. It'll be in cannon range by early evening. They have the weather gage and twice our guns in their favour; we have manoeuvrability, a long artillery piece, and the unerring eye of Lady Fang in ours.*

*This far north, we'll have but a few hours of daylight by which to make ready. Augustus Danvers, our pilot, has been loaned out to Mr. Pettigrew, the first mate, to assist with the shoring up of defences, which has consigned me to the coxswain's position. A temporary promotion, but one that is most welcome.*

*Captain Bellamy weighs our odds at fifty/fifty. I think he's being generous, deliberately giving the men a false sense of hope. It would not be the first time he has honeyed our ears with exaggerations. Either way, the forthcoming battle will undoubtedly be worthy of song. But will it be a rousing chaunt of victory? Or a dirge of defeat?*

*We shall know soon enough...our pursuer draws near, and both*

*my hands are needed on the wheel.*
   *May the dawn find us upright and seaworthy.*
   *May this not be my final entry.*
   *May God have mercy on our souls.*
   *O.C.*


'And the sea shall give up her bounty, for she possesseth much, and we ask so little in return.'

It was one of Captain Bellamy's favourite axioms, words he was wont to spout in the face of tribulation, as though they were a form of prayer. Or perhaps it was a benediction, born of superstition and too much rum.

Oliver Chance had heard the saying nearly a hundred times since joining the pirate crew, and yet it still carried an unmistakable weight of profundity. Of veracity. As if the words were a glimpse into the true workings of the vasty universe. Or mayhap it was simply because Bellamy's ship, Lacuna, was currently hundreds of leagues from the nearest landmass—and on the cusp of battle to boot—a situation which lent any lengthy sentence a degree of prophetic heft. Either way, he nodded dutifully, promptly agreeing with the captain's words, profound or otherwise. Like any loyal sailor should.

'Fair to say,' Oliver replied, tumultuous surf throwing salty spray over the railing, coating his tongue and stinging his eyes. 'Though it surely couldn't hurt to ask her to ease up on the white caps, if only just a little.'

The source of the churning waves, a black squall several miles off the starboard bow, had descended an hour earlier, darkening the skies and agitating the ocean with unbridled fury. Such foul weather would bear its own set of complications. It was anyone's guess which would catch up with the Lacuna first, the frigate or the storm, though Oliver's bet was on the squall.

Captain Bellamy gave a hearty bellow, a sound more akin to the roar of some wild animal, and clapped Oliver on the shoulder. Pain lanced across the younger man's back. For such an aged fellow, the captain possessed a heavy hand. That detail, in and of itself, was hardly a surprise—pirates didn't live to a ripe old age by being feeble. A fact that was doubly true for Captain Bellamy. For all his years, he was still as hard as a coffin nail, and his soul twice as black. 'Nay, let the sea buck and quiver, just like a proper ladylove. Those are the jaunts that we remember most fondly, are they not?'

The bawdy turn of phrase meant the captain was in the very best of moods, storm and pursuer be damned. Oliver was grateful for the good humour. A mercurial man at the best of times, Bellamy's abrupt changes in disposition were legendary, an ebb and flow of emotion which made him a difficult master to serve. One never knew which version of the captain would be emerging on deck at any given time. He could be of blustery temperament one minute, violent and querulous, and then astoundingly generous the next, like the sun emerging from behind grey clouds. As warm as a cookfire.

Behind the wrinkles and gray beard, however, lay a sharp and calculating mind, unspoiled by the passing of time.

The crew had many guesses for Bellamy's inconstant nature, suppositions whispered amongst themselves whilst swabbing the deck or mending rigging. A whole host of reasons both plausible and not. For his part, Oliver suspected that the captain's unpredictable moods were little more than an act, a sham designed to keep his crew on their toes. A tool employed to keep his captaincy unassailable.

But, if the captain was being lusty, it meant he was happy indeed. As though they had a fat merchantman in front of them instead of a ship-of-the-line in their wake. He was even wearing his brightest finery for the occasion: a red brocade jacket and brown leather breeches, both chased in silver.

'That they are, sir,' Oliver concurred, holding fast to the ship's wheel, keeping the Lacuna steady atop the roiling waves. He could agree with the captain's perspective if not the particulars thereof. Oliver preferred his partners to be a little more...masculine. Misters instead of mistresses. It was a predilection which he kept to himself—pirates were a largely tolerant bunch, but some things went too far beyond the pale, even for a boatload of brigands.

The only person on board who knew his secret was Lady Fang, the ship's sole female crewmember. They weren't lovers, naturally, but she seemed to hold him in some regard. Her real name, Xiang Yi Sao, was far too difficult for Lacuna's largely European crew to pronounce, resulting in the Anglicized bastardization. Nevertheless, it was a fitting sobriquet. Nobody knew quite where Captain

Bellamy had found the Chinese sharpshooter, or why such an exotic beauty abided a life of petty piracy. What *was* known, however, was her competence with a long-bore musket. It was a widely held belief aboard Lacuna that she had yet to miss a shot. Situated on the mainsail's fighting top, a sturdy platform affixed ten feet above the deck, Lady Fang was preoccupied with loading her rifles, bespoke flintlocks she allowed no other hands to touch. Once the fighting commenced, she would use her vantage point to snipe targets of opportunity at distance, primarily officers and seamen manning the frigate's swivel guns. Doing her part to sow discord and even the odds before the fighting began in earnest.

Bellamy's other secret weapon was the field artillery piece he called "Equalizer". Perched atop a purpose-built recoil carriage secured to the quarterdeck, the gun was more howitzer than proper cannon, barrel three times longer than those of Lacuna's broadside armament. It was an unwieldy weapon, good for only a handful of medium-range volleys at most. Terrifying and loud, the howitzer would open the engagement, lashing out at the enemy's rope and sail.

Lacuna would need all the help it could get: their pursuer was built for war, half again the size of Bellamy's ship, bristling with cannon and ill intent. Righteousness incarnate. Far worse, however, was the fact that the Navy frigate commanded the weather gage, an upwind positioning bestowing significant tactical superiority. Ships that controlled the weather gage controlled the skirmish itself.

Or so Oliver had been told. He was still learning the ins and outs of naval warfare, though his experiences had thus far been singularly one-sided. Pirates preyed on the weak and defenceless: merchant vessels, private ketches, and the like, most of which were lightly armed...if they were armed at all. Seabound raiders like Bellamy avoided stand-up engagements whenever possible, as the risks far outweighed any potential gains. What few battles Oliver had participated in were alacritous affairs, over nearly as soon as they'd begun.

Not to mention bloody, terrifying, and decidedly unscrupulous.

But he had learned much aboard the Lacuna, knowledge he hoped to put to use commanding his own vessel in the future. His educated background gave him a leg up over most of the crew, especially since he could read and write as well as comprehend sea charts and maps. All he had to do was learn the rest of it; the day-to-day operations of a ship itself, and the more esoteric aspects of commanding subordinates.

The last bit was proving difficult. Bellamy wasn't overly forthcoming with counsel, and his frequent mood swings made his mannerisms difficult to decipher. Nevertheless, several weeks after departing Algiers, he *had* offered up one piece of sound advice. While deep in his cups, the captain defined, rather succinctly, a pirate commander's greatest virtue.

'It's not about who's strongest,' Bellamy had said, his words frequently interrupted by vigorous rum-induced belches, 'nor is it about who commands the most powerful ship, or even who has the most loyal crew. A great pirate captain lives or dies by two factors, and two factors alone. Intelligence and ruthlessness.'

Given the captain's capricious nature, Oliver had witnessed ample instances of the latter. Generous moments aside, the older man's wrath was a frightening thing to behold. Like a put-upon father with too many unruly children, his discipline was prompt and severe, doled out for even the slightest infraction. Bellamy's aptitude was also without question—he excelled in the fields of seamanship, administration, and strategy, along with numerous, tangentially related endeavours. The kind of pirate a lad could look up to.

If anyone could see them through a scrape with the British Royal Navy, it was he.

Hours passed, somehow interminably slow and yet gone in a flash. Lacuna's crew waited, anticipative, muscles taut and brows glistening. The stink of unwashed bodies could not be completely dispelled by the wind. As for the squall, it had lost some of its potency, and was currently holding a mile abreast of the ships, content with being a spectator instead of a participant. The frigate, on the other hand, loomed large at their eight o'clock, still gaining despite her size. Oliver couldn't help but glance over his shoulder every few minutes, gauging the distance. While he watched, additional sails unfurled from the Navy ship's mizzen, seizing gusts of air like greedy children grasping for sweets. The craft seemed to be nothing but canvas—no wonder she was so swift.

Lacuna was still beyond the reach of the frigate's chase armament, but the same could not be said for their foe. The time had come to use the big gun. As per the captain's shouted orders, the topside gun crew loaded chain-shot into the howitzer's bore, two medium-sized iron balls fastened together by a length of chain. Such ammunition was designed to shred canvas and tack, though they made for ruinous anti-personnel rounds in a pinch.

'Keep her straight and sure, lad. We'll only get two shots at that behemoth, three if we're lucky,' Bellamy called to Oliver as the gun crew signalled ready, heavy winds nearly ripping the words away.

Those same winds, along with the pitching of the deck, would wreak havoc on the gunners' accuracy, altering the trajectory of projectiles in unpredictable ways. Targeting with "Equalizer" would be more an exercise in guesswork as opposed to an exhibition of actual skill. In spite of the long range, however, it would only take one lucky hit to foul up the Navy vessel's rigging. Maintaining speed at sea was a balancing act, the positioning of each sail receiving constant adjustment based on the ever-changing weather conditions—even minor damage could prove devastating to a ship's handling, rendering her, sometimes quite literally, dead in the water.

Oliver nodded tersely, shoulders squared, wheel held in a vice-like grip. He could feel his insides turning to liquid, as they always did just before a fight, but he tamped down on his fear. 'Aye, Captain! Steady as she goes!'

A minute went by. Then another. Twin booms sounded from behind, echoing off the waves, washing over Lacuna's deck with a soft rumble: the frigate's chase cannons probing the distance. It was more an intimidation tactic than anything—an *amuse-bouche* before the true feast commenced. Both rounds of chain-shot fell well short, plunging into the sea with impotent splashes.

'Gun crew, on my mark!' the captain bellowed in response, clapping his hands over his ears. Lacuna's back end rose as they crested a wave, the artillery piece's muzzle lifting inch by inch. 'Make ready...set...FIRE!'

The howitzer belched smoke and flame, discharging its deadly payload downrange with a banshee shriek of superheated metal. The weapon's report was deafening, a wall of sound both felt *and* heard, like the anvil of God being struck directly overhead. As if the very sky had been rent asunder. Heavy recoil flung the gun violently backwards in its carriage, wood and rope moaning from the strain.

Lacuna's quarterdeck shuddered under the impetus, not designed to weather the transference of so much energy.

Oliver glanced back at the frigate, searching for damage, but was unable to tell if they had hit or not. Judging by the curses expelled from behind the captain's prodigious beard, the shot must have gone wide.

'Reload!' Bellamy snarled, smacking the rear of the howitzer with an open palm.

Several tense minutes later, the gun was ready to fire once more. Again, the captain called out, and again Lacuna bucked under the intense knockback.

This time, however, a great cheer of *huzzah!* rose up from the deck, and Oliver could see one of the frigate's sails flying free in one corner, its rigging shredded and loose. The ship veered slightly to the left before her helmsman was able to compensate. In answer, the enemy craft loosed shot of their own. One of the rounds missed, whizzing harmlessly to port, but the other struck high, ripping a gaping hole in Lacuna's mainsail. Oliver could feel the loss of speed immediately, their momentum sloughing away as the sail became next to useless. Crippled as they were, the other ship would be upon them in minutes.

Captain Bellamy looked upwards, shaking his head in resignation. 'Well, that's that. It's to be broadsides and musket fire, then. So be it. Whatever happens, lad, do not let go of the wheel.'

'Aye, Captain!' Oliver affirmed. A lump had formed in his throat, but he swallowed it down, attempting to put on a brave face. From her perch on the fighting top, Lady Fang's eyes met his, and she gave a single nod of acknowledgement. She then raised a musket to her shoulder, sighting down the barrel with practised ease.

Eventide arrived with little fanfare, the sun disappearing beyond the horizon like an ill omen. Shadows skulked across the deck, forcing Oliver to blink furiously, willing his eyes to adjust. He would need his wits about him—ship-to-ship combat was a complicated dance at the best of times—an engagement by twilight would be nothing short of absolute chaos. Haphazard and disorientating.

Leaning over the quarterdeck railing, Captain Bellamy shouted downwards, his voice carrying across the entirety of the ship.

'Starboard battery, fire at will!'

Moments later, the Navy frigate drew up alongside, and Oliver's whole world seemed to erupt in fire and smoke, in splinters and screams. Both ships fired their broadsides simultaneously, iron cannonballs tearing into each other's hulls as though talons through hide. Lacuna jolted under each impact. Thump! Thump, THUMP! Muskets and swivel guns joined the barrage soon thereafter, lead balls whistling through the air with fervid indifference, lodging themselves within planking, rope, and flesh. Screams filled the night, as did the acrid scent of gunpowder and the copper tang of blood. Miles from their homes, atop unclaimed waters and floating wooden islands, the dead and the dying made their sacrifice.

Every instinct within Oliver was screaming for him to take cover. To hide. To escape the maelstrom of carnage that surrounded him. Yet he stood fast, knuckles white on the wheel, knees knocking together, body flinching with each near miss. A wretched soul amidst the cacophony of Hell itself. He adjusted course as per the captain's orders, unwavering gaze fixed firmly ahead, wilfully relegating the battle to the periphery. By the light of the stars, his watering eyes could just make out the lithe form of Lady Fang as she bent to her task, firing and swapping muskets with mechanical precision.

A haze of gun smoke shrouded the battlefield, obscuring all but the closest of details. Were they winning? Losing? Oliver had no way of knowing. It was only when the frigate veered sharply away (Lady Fang having struck the pilot, a hell of a shot through smoke and darkness) that he realized the Lacuna had emerged victorious.

A great cheer went up amongst the surviving crew as the enemy vessel fell behind, and Oliver breathed a sigh of relief. It was over.

'Give them another taste of artillery, lads!' Captain Bellamy urged; voice hoarse with bloodlust. 'See if we can't discourage them from following us further.'

He sidled up next to Oliver, throwing an arm around the younger man's shoulders. 'Well, lad, you survived your first proper sea battle. You're a veteran now, and no mistake. Invigorating, is it not?'

Oliver, muscles going slack as the tension left his body, could find no adequate words in response. All he could muster was a dry croak. His body felt numb through and through, a husk devoid of all earthly sensation. The wetness on his cheeks could very well have been from ocean spray. It was what he would claim, at least, should anyone have cause to ask. Such tears were unbecoming of a pirate, that much was certain. But he was powerless to stop them.

To his left, the howitzer boomed once more, discharging its lethal parcel into the night. Ruthlessness made manifest. The very trait the captain had espoused, all those nights prior, before the spectre of Death had descended upon the Atlantic with bloodied scythe and black-toothed grin.

#

November 20th, 1717
Brigantine Lacuna
Arctic Sea
250~ miles north-east of Greenland

*Light winds from the south-west; ship making 6 knots at best; crew are in poor temperament.*

*3000 miles we've tracked since departing Algiers—west, north, and occasionally east—the captain making haphazard course adjustments to throw off any pursuit, beholden as much to his whims as the capricious winds. 3000 gruelling miles...and nothing to show for it but a depleted roster and a tally of damages as long as my forearm.*

*I cannot say for certain whether the Navy frigate still hunts us, but Bellamy is taking no chances. Considering the throttling we received at the hands of that ship, one can hardly blame him, though I am fairly certain that she was barely seaworthy after the skirmish.*

*We are in the vast uncharted north now—icebergs litter the sea like floating cairns. The temperature hovers just above freezing. Hoarfrost is our constant companion: on spars, on anchor and chain, on weaponry. There is no daylight to be found, no sunrise with which to herald a new day. Only an incessant night-time that blackens the crew's already dismal spirits. Were it not for the occasional appearance of the northern lights, we would have no skyward illumination whatsoever, save for the stars themselves.*

*Captain Bellamy has become a recluse on his own ship, glimpsed only in passing, fleeting like the rats in our hold. As ephemeral as a phantom. I cannot fathom what is driving his behaviour, for it is most uncharacteristic. Guilt? Shame? Sickness? The answers elude me.*

*With more than half our crew dead or injured following our scrape with the frigate, the rest of us are obliged to pull double duty. First mate Pettigrew acts in the captain's stead, and, by attrition and popular vote, I have been officially commissioned as Lacuna's coxswain. I am learning much, though not in the easygoing manner I had initially hoped.*

*I know not what the captain seeks up here in the pack ice and the floes, but I do know that we are not provisioned for such an undertaking. Many of the men feel the same. There have been grumblings of mutiny—the notion if not yet the word itself—and I cannot say that I am utterly immune to the allure. The dangers of warfare are one thing; exposure and frostbite are something else entirely, invisible foes we are ill-equipped to face.*

*That we survived a sea battle only to succumb to the elements would be a bitter irony, indeed.*

*Captain Bellamy better have a damn good reason for such a risk.*

*O.C.*


'Bīngbiàn?' Lady Fang asked, reverting to her native tongue, though she did not seem aware of having done so. She understood English perfectly, yet rarely deigned to speak it. Her voice was high-pitched yet soft. When she noticed Oliver's confusion, she gave a slight cough before clarifying. 'Mutiny? Is that what you are proposing?'

Oliver's belly did a little dance, and he glanced around nervously. Just hearing the word spoken aloud made him fretful. They were situated in Lady Fang's suite, near the center of the ship on the portside. It was, in actuality, little more than a glorified closet, with hardly enough room for one person, let alone two. Especially with her assorted muskets nestled in one corner. But the suite was cozy in its own way, and smelt of soap and incense, along with more feminine elements. It even had a locking door. Moreover, it was private, being far removed from the crew's quarters, without even a porthole window through which to eavesdrop.

To Oliver, who slept in a hammock on the crowded gun deck,

surrounded by forty hygienically challenged men in hammocks of their own, Xiang's quarters were a little glimpse of heaven.

Xiang had changed from her usual black woollen attire into a blue silk robe, long black hair pulled up and bound by jade hair pins. Thin slippers adorned her feet, but her legs and arms were bare—the cold seemed to not be a bother at all. Within her quarters was the only time she dressed for comfort. Oliver, on the other hand, was garbed in his usual: fustian trousers and fearnought over a cotton shirt, with two pairs of stockings (for warmth) and leather boots.

'I propose nothing, Xiang,' he replied, grimacing slightly. 'I'm merely telling you what I've gleaned from the crew. The mood, the morale. Their despondency is so thick you can practically swim in it.'

It had been over a month since their battle with the Navy frigate. Lacuna may have survived, but she had taken quite a thrashing, holed through in multiple places. She was also woefully short on spares. The hull and mainsail had been patched, but they had lost the fore topsail, the fore staysail, and the jib. As such, Lacuna's speed and handling had been greatly diminished. Four of the seven starboard cannons had been destroyed, reduced to splinters and scrap by enemy projectiles. "Equalizer" was yet another casualty of the fray, and had been thrown overboard in order to reduce the ship's weight, much to the dismay of the gunners. Hundreds of feet of rigging had been damaged as well, forcing the crew to make do with bedsheets and cloth. The ship looked more patchwork than purposeful, but there was nothing for it.

Far worse, however, was the loss of men. Of the eighty-eight souls that had departed Algiers, twenty-seven had perished in the skirmish, with another nine dying of their wounds afterwards. Four had severe enough injuries that they were bedridden, and one was simply missing, presumed to have gone overboard during the conflict.

Which left forty-seven able-bodied men remaining. Less than fifty sailors to crew Lacuna, most of whom were trapped in the doldrums of grief and dread. Under normal circumstances, even a troupe of twelve could manage to sail a brigantine with reasonable seamanship. But, owing to the makeshift repairs and cold conditions, more hands than usual were needed to keep Lacuna on track.

'And the captain?' she asked, almond eyes boring into his own.

Oliver shrugged, glancing away. 'I've not seen him. Only those of his inner circle are allowed in his wardroom, and what is discussed in there, I cannot say. I don't like secrets, Xiang. Yet we find ourselves beset by them, even in the midst of the most hazardous conditions on earth. And here I thought Bellamy and I were friends. Of a sort, at least.'

Xiang placed a slender hand upon Oliver's knee, an unexpectedly intimate gesture from the generally reserved foreigner. Her accent caused her words to sound thick. Syrupy. But underneath the language barrier lay a gentleness, the likes of which was rare amongst ravagers and brigands.

'Such thinking is folly, *xiōngdì*,' she replied, using the nickname she had bestowed upon him months prior: the Chinese word for brother. 'A man like Bellamy has no friends. Only subordinates, rivals, and prey. You would do well to be none of them.'

'To be certain, but how do you suggest I go about that?'

'Perhaps the voices of the despondent could speak loudest of all? If called to do so?'

Oliver cocked his head to the side, trying to decipher her implication. 'What do you mean, Xiang?'

Before she could answer, there came a knock at the door. Both clamped their mouths shut in unison, as though they were a pair of co-conspirators who had just been discovered propounding treason. Which, on the face of it, was not far from the truth.

It was a rare occasion indeed when Lady Fang spoke so much all at once. And she never said anything if it wasn't important, which meant that her choice of words, however perplexing they might seem, were also deliberate. Had she been speaking of a vote? Most senior positions aboard a pirate ship were filled by popular election, even the captaincy. It was not uncommon for changes of leadership to occur, sometimes quite violently, during dire situations.

Oliver could hardly deny that the general attitude aboard Lacuna was...contentious. Patience was short, tempers were flaring. Pirates could be a fickle bunch, but they weren't stupid. Nor were they apt to spend their lives needlessly. A promise of great treasure was enticing, to be sure, but a man needed to be alive in order to spend such wealth. Plus, nobody knew what the captain's "great prize" was. Or if they'd even find it. As far as most pirates were concerned, they'd rather go after the easy money than chase a maybe. One in the hand was worth two in the bush, as the saying went. And, in that moment, the crew had naught in their hands at all.

The atmosphere was rife for a change, that much could not be argued. But was he willing to be the instigator of such reform? Now that was the real question.

'Captain's called a meeting, Mr. Chance,' called the voice of Henry Davidson, the ship's cook. He was another of Oliver's confidantes, level-headed and staunch. What the man thought of Oliver and Xiang's friendship was anyone's guess: he'd never said, and Oliver had never asked. 'All officers to the wardroom.'

Xiang leaned forward, dropping her tone to a whisper. 'We shall speak more on this later.'

#

To say that the atmosphere within the captain's quarters was strained was an understatement. Oliver could have cut the tension with a boat knife, had he been so inclined. Not that drawing a weapon within the captain's quarters would have been an advisable course of action, thick air or no.

Captain Bellamy had changed drastically within a month's time, to the point where he appeared sickly. Frail even. His already thin frame had gone gaunt, clothing hanging from him as if from a skeleton. Oliver spied bandages beneath the captain's cotton collar, indicative of wounds received during the battle, a condition which had been kept from the crew. Injuries were difficult to keep confidential aboard an ocean-going vessel; that the captain and surgeon had managed to do so was both impressive and disconcerting. Nevertheless, it went a long way in explaining the captain's truancy.

And yet, Oliver couldn't help but wonder if there was more to Bellamy's absence than mere battlefield lacerations. Such injuries were far from uncommon for the likes of pirates. Perhaps the man was also afflicted by a deteriorating mental state, as sometimes happened to people when they aged, their minds falling to entropy whilst their bodies weakened. Oliver was no doctor, of course, but he could tell that the captain was beset by some manner of malady.

94

In spite of his obvious infirmity, however, Bellamy's voice had lost none of its vigour.

'I thank you, gentlemen, for attending. We have much to discuss, so let's get right to it, shall we?'

There were grumblings of assent from everyone present: first mate Pettigrew, bosun Chisholm, sailing master Whitworth, surgeon Walsh, and master gunner Lockwood. Oliver would not normally have been invited to such a meeting, but his promotion to coxswain had placed him squarely within the ranks of principal officers.

Compared to Xiang's suite, the captain's wardroom felt palatial. Oliver could count on one hand the number of times he had been allowed to set foot inside. The space smelled of tobacco and all manner of spirits: rum, brandy, and other more earthy scents with which Oliver was unfamiliar. A host of creature comforts were arrayed throughout, including a large oaken desk, several bookshelves, a washbasin, and even a gilded chair. Sea charts littered the desktop, along with maritime implements for navigation. Oliver yearned to pore over the maps and papers, but he kept his gaze firmly on the captain, lest Bellamy take umbrage at such a breach of decorum.

'There are some who say that our time, the time of the pirates, is coming to an end. That the unceasing march of civilization will push us out, year by year, as the edges of the map are filled in. That we will have no place in this newly domesticated world, where the wild lands and untamed seas are no longer thus.'

There was a round of laughter around the table, dispelling the tension as though a lantern in a darkened room. Pettigrew slapped his knee with unfeigned mirth, while Lockwood wiped tears from the corner of his eyes. Bellamy, generally the most boisterous man aboard, did not join in merriment, however. Oliver watched the captain closely, searching his craggy and inscrutable face for some hint of the man's thoughts.

'These same men insist that we buccaneers are destined to be misremembered by history,' the captain continued, waving the men to silence. 'That our deeds are to be romanticized and our ferocity softened, much like the knights of yore. Did you know that, originally, knights were nothing more than thugs and well-provisioned bandits? They took what they wanted, and killed anyone who tried to stop them. Chivalry, that esteemed trait, was never intended to be a virtue of aspiration. Not initially, leastways. It was only thrust upon them in order to quell their violent tendencies. To keep them in check. And this, my friends, is the same fate these men insist is waiting for us.'

The first mate scoffed heartily, making his opinion on the subject plain. 'Surely they can't be right about that.'

'Ah, but they *are* right, Mr. Pettigrew. In my heart of hearts, I know it to be true. That frigate we duelled is but a taste of what is to come. Our way of life is dying, men. As surely as our brothers perished upon this very ocean.'

All traces of cheer died out, the assembled coterie settling back into their seats, adopting sombre countenances once more.

'If that is true, Captain, then what is our recourse?' queried Walsh, the most educated man aboard, and a damn fine practitioner of medicine as well.

The captain leaned forward, resting his elbows upon the table. Oliver couldn't help but mimic the action, his curiosity, as well as his unease, growing by the minute. The room had gone so silent that a dropped pin would have sounded like thunder. 'Our recourse is quite simple, doctor. We make our fortune, and we retire to a life of ease and quiescent iniquity. Let the world move on...we shall live as kings until old age claims us, far from the eyes of those who would see us hanged.'

Pettigrew was nodding vigorously, as though he were in on the secret, while Chisholm covered a cough with the back of his hand. 'Simple, you say? Not to sound sceptical, sir, but I'm assuming you have a plan for how to accomplish such a trick?'

'I do, indeed. And it is time to share that scheme with the assembly, since most of you are relatively new additions to Lacuna's complement. Two years ago, almost to the day, in point of fact, first mate Pettigrew and I chased a Dutch merchantman into these very waters. HNLMS Bliksem, translated from the Dutch as "Lightning", had led us on a merry chase, being a barque of particularly sleek design. Up and down the Atlantic she fled, with us never less than a day behind. She may have been faster, but we had skill on our side. Seamanship will win out over speed in nearly every instance. Of course, we were also buoyed by a burning hunger for the wealth she was carrying. And I don't mean the usual cargo of spices, silks, sugar, and furs. No, Bliksem was ferrying legitimate treasure, a cache of pilfered riches from Morocco: gold, silver, and gemstones.'

All the things that a pirate craved, thought Oliver. Though many pirate crews boasted of liberating similar treasures from the holds of unlucky vessels, such finds were, in all actuality, exceedingly rare. Tall tales of legend used to lure new recruits and entice ladies to doff their garments. But if Bellamy had actually found such a ship... The change in the room was palpable, greed overtaking doubt in the blink of an eye. Oliver, for his part, tried to remain objective. It was no easy feat.

'Of course, the Dutch crew had no interest in being caught,' the captain persisted, eyeing each man in turn. 'Straight into the floes she went, navigating further and further north, through channels almost too narrow for Lacuna. And then, before we could catch her, the ocean froze over, stranding her. Would have stranded us as well, but we turned back south before the ice could claim us.'

Minutes passed as each man mulled the story over. Oliver did not doubt the veracity of the story, but even so, he could not contain his pessimism. 'And so, you intend for us to find this ship once more, risking the same dangers you faced two years ago? In darkness, with only a vague notion of where she may be resting?'

A dark look flashed across Bellamy's eyes, and Oliver swallowed hard, realizing he may have been a little too brusque with his query. But there was no taking it back. The rest of the crew were nodding in agreement, however. All save Pettigrew, who scowled in Oliver's direction, his mien one of frank animosity.

'No, lad. I have it on good authority that a large section of pack ice has broken free from the main body, the currents carrying it southward, conveying with it a stranded ship. A three-masted barque of Dutch design, as it so happens. We need not scour the boundless frozen north for her at all. Bliksem, crewed only by frozen bodies and unanswered prayers, will come to us.'

#

November 27th, 1717
Brigantine Lacuna

97

Arctic Sea
280~ miles north-east of Greenland

*Light winds from the east; ship anchored and sails furled; crew are agitated and intemperate.*

*We have arrived at the promised sheet of pack ice, as spotted by lookouts in the crow's nest, though two more men were lost to exposure along the way. That great frozen plateau, and the vessel trapped within, is slowly drifting away from its brethren, albeit without much hurry. I estimate it to be travelling at less than two knots.*

*Frostbite has claimed more of the crew's fingers and toes than I would like to admit, and even a few noses as well. The men have been whispering amongst themselves, and I can feel lines being drawn, sides being taken.*

*What's more, our stores are running low. Food, lantern oil, and fresh water are nearly depleted. Mr. Davidson has been doing his best to stockpile and ration, but is afraid of causing a panic.*

*Undeterred by objections—from myself and several others—the captain, along with a handful of his loyalists, departed in Lacuna's jolly boat during first watch, taking with them a makeshift sledge. They intended to beach alongside the ice, then march overland to Bliksem, hauling whatever treasure they could find back behind them. Captain Bellamy insisted the trek would take no more than three days...five have passed, yet we've seen and heard nothing. I cannot say that I am surprised: all the zeal in the world is no substitute for cold weather paraphernalia.*

*First mate Pettigrew stayed behind, as per the captain's command. It is clear that he is to act as chaperone, holding Lacuna at her position, keeping order until Bellamy's return. But in this task, he is failing; watching their compatriots be taken by the elements, all for the "possibility" of a great recompense, is taking a heavy toll.*

*The crew will not abide another day in this godforsaken place.*

*Which is just as well. The ocean to our north is freezing over, ice encroaching upon our position with each passing hour as the temperature plummets, the sea succumbing to winter's embrace. If we do not depart presently, we are sure to suffer the same terrible fate as Bliksem.*

*A mutiny is soon to erupt. Who will survive such an upheaval, I wonder?*

*For my part, I cannot bear to see any more of my friends perish. What if it's Mr. Davidson next? Or Xiang, heaven forbid?*

*No, I feel compelled to take action, and therefore action I shall take.*

*I would pray, but I fear that God is not listening.*

*O.C.*


Oliver ascended the steps onto Lacuna's deck at noon, six days after Captain Bellamy's hazardous excursion. Lady Fang accompanied him, armed with her favorite musket, though she veered away once they were topside. She would watch from a distance, she had said. The rest was up to him, as they had discussed.

Darkness prevailed, the sun not having risen in weeks. Of the three men on watch, one was fast asleep, swaddled in blankets, whilst another stared off into the distance, barely conscious. Only the sailor on the foredeck, a Mr. Spurlock, seemed coherent. Pettigrew stood fast on the quarterdeck, a single hand on the ship's bittacle, looking pensive. Great gusts of steam blew from his mouth, swirling in the frigid air. He spared Oliver a passing glance before turning his gaze to the pack ice once more.

Making his way to the windlass, Oliver could hear other crewmen climbing onto the deck. In spite of their thinned ranks, there were still plenty of mouths to blather, and rumours passed through a ship like wildfire. The crew knew something was about to transpire, and there was no way they were going to miss it.

For Oliver, his mind was pulled in several directions at once. He understood what he had to do, and yet his thoughts were chaotic, maudlin even, slewing towards a level of sentiment he had never before experienced. How long had it been since he'd felt warm? Since he had heard the call of gulls, or squinted as the sun crested the horizon? Oliver was finding it difficult to recall a time before everything was covered in frost and misery.

'Alright, men,' he declared, glancing around as more and more sailors joined them, while the northern lights danced overhead, casting a sickly pall across the faces of those assembled. As though his exhortation was to be presided over by ghosts. Walsh was in

99

attendance, as was Chisholm. Whitworth and Lockwood had accompanied the captain and were surely never to return. 'I don't know about you, but I think it is time to call this fool's errand a bust. Are we in agreeance?'

There were rumblings of assent, and a couple of the men muttered "aye", while more than a few cast fearful glances towards the first mate. Oliver sighed with exasperation. The crew weren't as motivated as he had hoped, the chill having leached the very spirit from their bones. He would need to try harder.

'Well, that was about as lackluster a response as I've ever heard, and I once tutored at a seaside charity school. Shall we give it another go? I asked, are we done freezing our arses off for nothing in return?'

This time, every man in attendance responded, nodding his head and shaking his fists. 'Aye!' came the rejoinder, loud and clear.

'Very well. Spurlock,' Oliver called out, injecting as much authority into his voice as he could muster. 'Weigh anchor. It is high time we made our way back to the sun.'

Spurlock paused for a moment, glancing between Oliver and Pettigrew, before stammering a response. 'I, uh...yes, sir. Anchor aweigh.'

'You *will* belay that order at once, Mister Chance!' screamed Pettigrew, stalking across the deck with a *clomp clomp* of heavy boots, shouldering past the crew to stand directly in front of Oliver. The first mate was the taller man by at least six inches, broader around the chest, with arms as thick as cannon barrels. The very picture of intimidation, as warranted by his assignation.

Oliver swallowed painfully but stood his ground, meeting Pettigrew's gaze without blinking. 'No, sir, I shall not.'

The first mate pulled a flintlock pistol from his belt, pointing it squarely between Oliver's eyes. 'You will belay that order, pilot.' The pistol's barrel was akin to a great void, a deep and vasty blackness that threatened to swallow Oliver's soul. He had to fight the urge to soil himself, but somehow found the courage to stand tall.

'Nay, Mr. Pettigrew. Nay. We joined this crew to plunder riches and live free, not to perish needlessly in some frozen hellscape.'

'Hear, hear!' yelled a few of the men, and Oliver could see realization dawning in the first mate's eyes. The situation was about to spiral out of control, and he only had the one shot. Even still, Pettigrew kept doggedly on, clinging to maxims out of tremulous desperation.

'Our captain ordered us to stay here until his return,' he squawked, Adam's apple bobbing nervously, 'and I for one intend to follow that order! Even if it means that I die here, borne atop the salty sea, as God intended.'

Oliver spat, vexation at the other man's idiocy overriding his fear. 'The captain is dead, man! Dead! He is NOT coming back. And God is nowhere to be found this day, for even He fears the barrenness of this hateful place.'

'No,' the first mate responded, shaking his head, 'No, Captain Bellamy is not dead.' Pettigrew thumbed back the hammer, priming his weapon, unsteady hand causing the barrel to shake erratically. 'I am going to count to three, and if you don't retract that order, I will shoot you where you stand!'

'Then you're going to have to shoot me,' Oliver replied, closing his eyes.

An expectant hush descended upon the deck, and even the breeze seemed to still, as though the whole world wished to bear witness. Pettigrew's pistol barrel pressed against his forehead, burning like frozen fire. Oliver sighed, saddened by his impending death, but secure in the knowledge that it would spur the men to action. That his sacrifice would not be in vain. The crew would overpower Pettigrew and flee the Arctic Ocean, of that much he was certain. They would be saved, as would Xiang. It would have to be enough.

'One,' said Pettigrew, voice brittle and wavering.

Sucking in a breath, Oliver allowed his mind to wander, recalling happier days. His thoughts turned to Samuel, a handsome lad he had met one wistful summer day, one who possessed the most captivating eyes Oliver had ever seen. It was far too late for what could have been, but he indulged in a fancy or two, all the same.

'Two,' the first mate counted, more plea than threat.

Oliver clenched his fists, his back held ramrod straight. He'd be damned if he would give Pettigrew any semblance of satisfaction in his final moments.

'Thr...'

A shot rang out, as loud as cannon fire in the crisp northern air, and Oliver's eyes flashed open. He felt no pain, no heat. No forceful impact against his forehead. The gunshot sounded distant, elevated, though he attributed that detail to shock more than anything. It was only when Pettigrew stumbled and toppled sideways, blood bubbling from his lips, that Oliver realized the truth. The stocky first mate slipped over the railing, hitting the water with a resounding splash. Oliver glanced upwards, eyes searching in the low light. From her vantage point on the fighting top, Lady Fang slowly lowered her long-bore, the muzzle still smoking. She gave a single nod in his direction, and then began climbing down the rigging to join him on deck.

Oliver had an overwhelming urge to feel his forehead, to make sure Pettigrew's death wasn't simply a delirium conjured by a damaged mind, but he resisted. Instead, he stared for a long moment at the railing where Pettigrew had pitched over. A collective sigh rose up from those assembled, an exhalation of pure assuagement. Oliver released his own pent-up breath, thoroughly astonished to be alive. But there was more amazement yet to come.

From the cluster of men, Henry Davidson's voice, coloured by both stupefaction and elation, sang out to the rest of the crew.

'Lacuna is without both a commander and a first mate, finding herself in the most dire of straits. I call a vote for captaincy.'

Oliver turned to face his friend, eyes wide with disbelief. The cook was grinning, the first smile to be seen on anyone's face in days. 'Henry, what are you...?'

'I hereby nominate Oliver Chance, coxswain and Lacuna's loudest voice of reason, as captain. All those in favour?'

'Aye!' came the fervent acknowledgement of the crew, their thunderous cry echoing across the frozen expanse. Lady Fang's voice was loudest of all, a singsong falsetto that reached deep into Oliver's heart to stoke the embers therein, warming him from the inside out.

'AYE!'

#

December 2nd, 1717
Brigantine Lacuna

Arctic Sea
300~ miles south-east of Greenland

*Strong winds from the east; ship making 8 knots; crew are in high spirits.*

*We have made good our escape, leaving the icy north abaft with nary a second glance. Through either luck or divine intervention, not another soul has been lost, though Lacuna is now woefully undermanned. We will need all of our wits and skill to avoid confrontation on our return journey to Algiers.*

*Repairs will be expensive; I shall have to sell off some of Bellamy's valuables in order to purchase the necessary supplies. I am also short on senior staff, and have been mulling over my nominations for the past few days, weighing options. I offered the first mate position to Xiang, which she refused most vociferously, though she was smiling as she declined. Perhaps she will warm to the idea over time.*

*It does not yet feel real, the crew calling me captain. I worry that I am dreaming, and shall awaken to find us still under Bellamy's command, senselessly chasing his Dutch barque, sailing straight towards certain death. I suspect that particular fear shall haunt my dreams for some time.*

*But dreams hold no dominion in the waking world; Lacuna is mine, and Bellamy is dead. I'll not squander this opportunity.*

*Captain Joseph Bellamy had his time.*

*Captain Oliver Chance has just been given his. I shall do it right, not chasing fancies like he did. And the sea shall give up her bounty, for she possesseth much, and we will ask so little in return.*

*O' lord, I do thank thee.*

*O.C.*

# DUNGEON ROCK

## Edward Lodi

If you really want to know, I'll tell you why. Why every Halloween I lock myself indoors with all the lights ablaze and a bottle of single malt whiskey by my side.

It wasn't always like this. From the time I was a little kid until well into adulthood, of all the days of the year October 31st was my favorite. As Scout Leader, every Halloween, weather permitting, I'd take my troop into the Saugus woods, where we'd build a fire, toast hotdogs and marshmallows, drink hot chocolate, and tell ghost stories. It was all innocent fun. The guys honed their survival skills, learning how to select a campsite, gather wood, the best way to build a fire without matches, and how to safely extinguish the embers before returning home.

It was a tradition we all looked forward to—until the year Bill Hartley volunteered to come along.

Bill was our self-appointed local historian. Every New England town, it seems, has one. He'd spent a good part of his life researching the history of Saugus, from the days of the earliest Puritan settlement, when Saugus was still part of Lynn, all the way up to and including the American Revolution. He knew all about the Indian Wars, King Philip's War and the French and Indian Wars that followed. And he knew the local legends, the persecutions of Quakers and Baptists, tales of buried treasure, witches, pirates, and the ghosts that haunt the area.

All the month of October Bill bugged me to allow him to tag along. 'C'mon, Joe,' he pleaded, tugging at my sleeve in front of Starbucks, where he waylaid me on my way to the drugstore. 'I know some great ghost stories. True stories, at least as far as the history goes.'

I tried to break away, but he wouldn't be put off. 'Kids nowadays spend too much time on gadgets,' he persisted, keeping up with me as I hurried along. 'Social media. It's not healthy. Besides, it's getting so nobody gives a damn about past events any more.'

Finally I gave in. I'd been reluctant, because, well, there'd been some ugly rumors. Bill's wife, Betty, had mysteriously disappeared the year before. Simply vanished. It was no secret that Bill was an abusive husband. Many a time Betty was seen with her eyes blackened and bruises on her face. She always denied there was anything wrong, but the townsfolk knew better.

Fortunately, the couple had no children. Some people gave Bill the benefit of doubt, assuming that Betty, sick and tired of being knocked around, had taken off. Others, though, had more sinister theories about what might have happened. Some even thought—well, there are a lot of woods, isolated spots, in the area, places where a body might be buried and never discovered.

From the outset, the police considered Bill a "person of interest" in his wife's disappearance. But nothing ever came of it.

I didn't think it was altruism that motivated Bill Hartley to volunteer as raconteur of ghost stories. He was, I thought, desperate to salvage whatever of his reputation remained. To be seen as a do-gooder, a nice guy in spite of what people thought. Or it's possible he just wanted to share with others the history and folklore of Saugus.

Anyhow, when Halloween came around I borrowed a van from The Council on Aging, and accompanied by Bill rounded up the scouts. Bill carried with him a backpack which contained, he told me in confidence, a pirate outfit. The story he intended to tell involved a pirate. After telling the story, he planned to slip away in the dark, put on the costume, and come back as the pirate's ghost.

'The kids won't really be scared,' he assured me. 'They'll know it's me. Even so, it'll be fun.'

We arrived at the site I'd chosen a few days before—a clearing in the woods near the coast—an hour before nightfall, allowing time for the guys to gather a sufficient amount of dried twigs and fallen tree limbs to last the evening. Josh Mendoza, who was on track to becoming an Eagle Scout, showed the less experienced boys how to build the fire, and how to help put it out if it got out of hand.

We were lucky regarding the weather. Though a stiff breeze blew in from the Atlantic, the tall conifers that crowded onto the edges of the clearing softened the brunt. The moon, on the wane, together with flames from the campfire provided just enough light for us to see one another, but not enough to prevent the younger kids from casting apprehensive looks over their shoulders now and then at the surrounding dark. Swift moving clouds scudding across the face of the moon added to the spookiness.

The fresh air spiked everyone's appetite. Once the flames grew hot and embers formed, the boys got a kettle going. With steaming mugs of hot chocolate by our side, we skewered hotdogs on the ends of freshly whittled twigs and dangled them over the open fire. Bill waited until everyone had eaten at least one hotdog before beginning his story.

'As you have probably been told,' he said, staring at each of the boys one at a time, 'this area is haunted. And not just by one ghost, but by two.' He let that sink in. 'There are two facts you should know before I tell you how it all came about. In the Seventeenth century, a pirate by the name of Thomas Veale preyed upon ships along the New England coast. And in 1658 a powerful earthquake shook the whole of Massachusetts Bay Colony.'

The wind began to pick up. A sudden gust rustled through the trees, providing gratuitous sound effects.

'Some years before the earthquake, a small bark was seen to drop anchor near the mouth of the Saugus River.' He paused. 'Not all that far from here. A boat was lowered from its side. Four men got into the boat and rowed a short way upriver to the point where the river meets the hills. The men tied the boat to a tree near the river bank and disappeared into the woods. The next day the boat was gone.

'But that morning a workman on his way to the iron forge—for which Saugus was then famous—found a note nailed to a tree. The note, which was unsigned, stated that if a specified number of shackles, handcuffs, and other items were made and left at a designated spot in the woods—some folks say this very spot where we're sitting—a generous number of Spanish silver dollars and pieces of eight would be left in the same spot.

'Workers at the ironworks, eager to earn the silver coins, made the items the pirates requested—for who else but pirates would require such items, and pay for them with Spanish silver? Leaving the items at the assigned spot, they kept a careful watch. But though no vessels were seen to approach the area, and they saw no one gather up the items, in the morning they were gone, and the promised silver left in their place.'

Bill had the kids' rapt attention. He paused to spear a hotdog and hold it over the campfire before continuing. 'Months later, the four pirates returned and established themselves in a remote area of Saugus. Remote then, but not now. Somewhere around here, I believe it was. This time, though, the pirate leader—the notorious Thomas Veale, scourge of the New England coast—brought with him a woman of extraordinary beauty. Whether she came willingly, or as a captive, none can say. What we do know is that folks passing through the area would sometimes hear a woman sobbing, and on a few occasions screaming, as if for mercy.'

Bill paused. What happened next was a coincidence. What other explanation can there be? As Bill left off his narrative to see how his hotdog was progressing, a scream not unlike that which he had just described pierced the night air. More of a bloodcurdling shriek than a mere scream, I think. I don't rightly remember, it so startled us.

If the scouts—and I include myself in their number—nearly wet their pants, the effect on Bill was far greater. With a start, he dropped the hotdog—still attached to the skewer—into the flames and leapt to his feet. He looked wildly about him, as if expecting Satan himself to appear.

'What was that?' he asked, in a tremulous voice.

By then I had somewhat collected myself. 'Must've been a screech owl,' I said, in as calm a voice as I could muster. I didn't for a moment believe it was a screech owl, but what else could it have been?

The night seemed to gather around us, though in truth it was probably an effect of clouds sliding across the moon. 'An owl,' Bill said. 'Of course. I was so engrossed in my story, it startled me. An owl, yes.' With shaking hands he reached for a hotdog, but changing his mind sat down again.

He took a moment to compose himself, then resumed his story. 'This went on—the woman heard sobbing, I mean—for several months. And then, strangely, she was neither seen nor heard again.

'What happened to her? Who knows? Did she pine away from

grief and despair? Did she sicken and die? Or did something more sinister happen? We'll never know. But there are folks who say her restless spirit wanders the area, and can be heard on nights such as these, when the wind howls through the trees and swiftly moving clouds race across the sky.'

He fell silent.

What possessed Bill to tell this story? I wondered, as we huddled around the leaping flames, which Josh fed from time to time with twigs and dried limbs. Was it a guilty conscience? Is that why Bill insisted on coming with us that night? Was it a veiled confession? Or was it an act of defiance? A signal that he didn't give a hoot (poor choice of words!) about what townsfolk might think of him.

'Great story, Bill,' I said. 'Hey guys, give Mr Hartley a round of applause.'

'Oh, but wait,' Bill said, holding up his hand. 'That's only half the story. I mentioned two ghosts, remember?'

'Gary,' I said to the youngest scout. 'Pass around the marshmallows so we can toast them while Mr. Hartley finishes his tale.'

'It was not long after the woman disappeared that a band of men raided the pirates' home. They caught three of the pirates, but the fourth—Thomas Veale—escaped. The three were taken to England to be put on trial for their dastardly deeds. There they were found guilty and hanged. As was the custom in those days, their bodies were displayed on gibbets and left to rot, for all to see and take warning.

'In the meantime, Veale established himself in a cave hidden in the woods, where he and his men stored the treasure they'd accumulated in the course of their nefarious career. Having fashioned a home of sorts deep within the cave, he resumed shoemaking, the trade he'd followed before becoming a pirate. Making and repairing shoes gave him an excuse to go into town whenever he needed supplies.

'However, he didn't practice shoemaking for long. In 1658 the powerful earthquake I mentioned caused the entrance to the cave to collapse, converting the cave into a dungeon, inside which Thomas Veale was sealed alive, along with his treasure. To this day the hill where the entrance to the cave was located is called Dungeon Rock.'

Bill paused to glance around the circle of eager faces. 'Dungeon Rock is a short walk from here. But don't bother to go looking for the treasure. People have been doing that for centuries, with no success. The treasure lies hidden deep within the bowels of the earth—along with Thomas Veale.

'Besides,' he added, 'Veale's vengeful ghost wanders these woods, and gets very upset if folks come snooping around.'

Rising to his feet, Bill stepped away from the fire as if to answer a call from nature, and crossed to the edge of the clearing and into the woods. He'd return shortly, I knew, decked out in his pirate costume to give the boys a scare. So far, I had to admit, the evening was a success. The scouts seemed to have enjoyed the story. In the short while between Bill's leaving and the pirate's appearance, they chatted away, teasing one another about being scared of the dark, while the bolder ones laid out plans for finding the treasure.

Sooner than I expected, Bill emerged from the shadows, on the opposite side of the clearing from where he'd left, and wordlessly approached. As soon as he stepped into view one or two of the kids let out a squeal of fright, while most of the others seemed transfixed, unable to move. I can't say I blame them. If I hadn't been expecting him, I'd have been frightened, too.

I have to say he'd outdone himself. Not only did he look like an authentic pirate, dressed in what I took to be typical sailor's garb of the Seventeenth century—and not like some outlandish cartoonish caricature—but more than that, even more impressive, the make-up he'd applied gave to his flesh a ghastly pallor, as if the corpse of Thomas Veale had broken free of its entombment in Dungeon Rock to seek vengeance on those who, on Halloween, dared to venture into his domain.

His appearance was brief. No sooner did he step into the clearing, than out he stepped again, into the shadows—the way I suppose a real ghost might manifest itself, then vanish, leaving witnesses to doubt whether what they had seen was real, or merely a figment of their imagination.

The boys sat and stared at one another. As if sensing the chill that we all felt, Josh heaped more fuel onto the fire, causing the flames to leap and dance like demons whipped into a frenzy (such were my thoughts at the time), yet making the night seem somehow darker, colder.

And then we heard a shriek, that same shriek we'd heard earlier, scarcely human in its intensity—followed by another shriek, this one a cry of anguish such as a man might make, a man in abject terror, being struck a mortal blow. Then the night fell silent, save for the wind, which whispered through the conifers, hinting at secrets only it was privy to.

While I waited for Bill to return, I encouraged the scouts to toast the remainder of the marshmallows before dousing the fire, and warm themselves with hot chocolate. It was almost time to pack up. We all had flashlights of course. Even so, it would take a while to make our way along the trail to where I'd parked the van, a half mile or so from the campsite. I didn't want to incur the ire of parents by bringing home the scouts later than promised.

Not all promises can be kept. Some delays are inescapable. Bill never returned.

When it became obvious that something was wrong—thinking that he must have lost his way—I had the kids holler 'Mr Hartley' at the top of their lungs.

To no avail. Bill wasn't within hearing distance. Or if he was, he was unable to respond. Having no alternative, I took out my cell phone and called 911. Explaining the situation, I gave our location as best I could.

'Hartley's out there somewhere,' I said. 'Possibly injured. I have to take the kids home, but as soon as I've done that I'll return.'

We searched all night but found no trace of Bill—other than his backpack, which was still lying where I'd seen him leave it the night before. The strange thing is, the pirate outfit he'd intended to wear was still inside.

It bore no resemblance to the one we'd seen on Thomas Veale when he made his brief appearance. The costume in the backpack was the kind you'd wear to a kids' Halloween Party. As for Bill, he was never seen again.

The theory held by most folks was that, having murdered Betty and disposed of her body, he decided to make a run for it before the police had a chance to establish his guilt and arrest him. The rigmarole he'd concocted about the pirate's ghost was just a ruse to throw people off the scent.

To me, that made no sense. His car was parked in the driveway where he lived. Nothing in the house was missing. He'd left everything, clothing included, behind. What money he had in the bank still sat there. And who in his right mind, intending to flee the law, would accompany a troop of Boy Scouts into the woods at night before taking off?

And how do you explain Thomas Veale's appearance in the clearing? It wasn't just me who saw him. The scouts did, too. My theory is that Bill Hartley's sins caught up with him. Those shrieks we heard. An owl? Or maybe...

Maybe it was the ghost of the woman Thomas Veale abused in the 1650s, the woman whose death he caused, whether intentionally or not, taking out her wrath on an abusive husband of the present day. Or maybe it was Betty Hartley's ghost. Maybe Bill had, after all, murdered his wife and buried her body out there in the woods. Maybe her spirit, freed on Halloween, had taken its revenge.

Or maybe Thomas Veale, cooped up all those centuries in the collapsed cave, all by himself in that dark dungeon, feeling lonely, had snatched up Bill—a kindred spirit—and dragged him there to keep him company.

Preposterous, you're probably thinking. The ranting of a man traumatized and shaken by what he perceives as an inexplicable occurrence. And no doubt you're right. There are no such things as vengeful spirits. No such things as ghosts. Even so, I, who am not without sin, no longer venture out on Halloween, but cower in my house with the lights all ablaze, and a bottle of Dutch courage by my side.

# THE AVERY DOG HAS HIS DAY
## Rose Biggin

The first truly great day of Henry Avery's life was the day he overthrew his captain. There had been fine times before, true enough: the day he took his first steps onto a ship as a boy, skulking about the harbour at Plymouth and already dreaming of wars and adventures on the sea; the days marked by success in naval battle, the smell of the smoke and the taste of his own precious life like clear water; and of course the all-day and all-night bout of drinking (going through into the next day, and all the following night) when he was promoted to first mate. But looking back, none of those counted. This was the day that made him who he was. It was the mid 1690s. The naval ship was anchored just outside a Spanish harbour when the rumblings of the crew reached a point of boiling, and when the violence broke out, oh, how it broke.

Avery stood firm on the deck, a spray of blood on his forearm, tight grip clutched onto the handle of his knife, pistol still raised having fired a triumphant shot into the air, and he listened to the chanting of the crew—*his* crew, now, for so they were—churning in his ears. The vote had been unanimous and it had been for him. The ship would have a new name, they would set a course for the Cape of Good Hope, and they would throw off the naval colours and see out the last few years of the seventeenth century with the glorious freedom of pirates.

Then they had to haul anchor very quickly because the gunships guarding the Spanish harbour, on receiving news of what was happening, began firing at them.

\#

Avery's next good day occurred a year into his career as a pirate, when he successfully chased down the biggest treasure ship he'd ever seen.

The heist had been tricky to arrange, requiring Avery to secure the cooperation of half a dozen pirate captains, each of whom required a different method of persuasion; this in itself was an achievement the others could respect and in the end they'd made him the Admiral, in charge of the whole damned lot.

The day was clear and bright, the pirate ships lying in wait among the Straits of Bab-el-Mandeb. The hours passed slowly in the effort of suspense and after a time Avery thought he could hear whisperings among his crew: were they in the right place? Had the treasure fleet learned of the plan, had they gone another route? Then, the sun high in the cloudless sky, lips cracking with the heat, he put his hand to his eyes and watched as the great convoy finally appeared, a huge mass of ships coming through the straits, a floating city. The treasure fleet was bigger than they'd all thought: what was that, two dozen ships, more? And each would be carrying twice the crew of Avery's entire fleet combined. And there, in the centre, the prize of prizes, the biggest treasure ship in the world, loaded with plunder and bristling with cannons, and behind was another, possibly even bigger, also with plenty of treasure, and certainly with even more cannons. Avery smiled, feeling the mutterings of his men give way to excited whispers, to preparations for sail. Had they gone another route, ha! There wasn't much hiding a great golden goose like that, not from Avery.

There would be fine moments to follow, after the initial day of chase: catching up and boarding the first treasure ship, dividing up the loot, shouting with laughter at the sheer size of the haul; hearing the news of his fellow captains' failures, shipwrecks, disasters, and caring only to continue on; reaching the next prize, the biggest in the world; calling instructions amidst the sound of musket-fire; the wooden sounds of his crew scrambling up the side of the ship; swinging aboard, the weight of the landing; looking into the captain's eye as he surrendered. These were fine moments, achievements the others would talk about, that his crew would sing about, that the crowned heads of the world would hurriedly order his urgent capture about. But for Avery, the thrill of that first day was a euphoria unsurpassed, giving chase and nothing else, and for a long time he feared he'd never recapture the joy of it; leaning out from the rigging, pulling on the rope, testing the balance of his own weight against the strength of the ship, feeling the air in his face with its tang of salt and screaming out in the rush, pressing for more speed, more, and the gap between his own ship and the treasure fleet narrowing, narrowing, narrowing.

\#

Henry Avery's third good day occurred a year or so later, when he successfully evaded capture and the rope and vanished.

Not even the sight of the gibbet, its shadows stretching out into the setting sun, could affect his spirits, once he knew this wasn't the fate for *him*. His crew had been caught, sped through a quick trial for the purpose of show and sentenced to hang for the crimes they had committed on the treasure fleet, and it was a mighty shame of an outcome, no doubt; but Avery hadn't been there to be caught, and he had gotten away, and he was going to make it so they never found him, nor the treasure neither; and as he pulled on the oars, making his way to a different life in the shadow of the death that awaited his former crewmates, he knew this was a blessed day for him.

\#

Avery's fourth and fifth good days came in quick succession, although they didn't start out well. The fourth, frankly, was set to be an awful day; it only had to be counted as a good one because he survived it. The issue was a fight, and not a fair one either. The eyes of those dodgy scoundrels in the corner should have been enough of a warning to him. He'd been on the run and in hiding for several years now—he'd seen out the 1690s, it was the early seventeen-hundreds, a whole new era for him—but he was still big, he still had the muscle; he could deal with any trouble, so he thought. He'd put his rum down and walked out without looking back. He'd expected them to follow, which they did, but he hadn't reckoned on there being a group of their friends also waiting outside.

They didn't know who he was—nobody did—so it must have

been purely for the fun of the violence, simply to say they had done it. What a disappointing way to go, Avery thought, and he thought it would be his last thought, as the world went dark around him.

Then, hours later, Avery slowly pulled himself from the muddy puddle where his body had been thrown. There was a horrible scraping of bones in his leg and hip and a grasping pain where his neck met his skull: but could it be the wounds, although delivered as fatal, weren't so deep after all? He gingerly sat up, then made a slow and agonising crawl into the foliage at the side of the path. They'd taken all the coin he carried and it was strange they'd let him live. Avery put a tentative hand to his throat. You don't cut like that without intending to kill. Yet he'd lived. This had to be what you'd call a good day. And the one after that, by the end of which his neck had completely healed, and so had all his other injuries, was a good day too.

#

Avery's sixth very good day, a few years later: the day he realised he could not die.

When his recovery from the attack by the inn was so much quicker than he would have expected, his confidence had grown; and he soon learned that no injury seemed to stick with him for long. This was a huge boon for a life that required so much risk, for he made his way in the world running petty enterprises and bargaining for smuggled things, a business fraught with the ever-present threat of sudden extreme reversals of fortune. Then, one day, he'd trodden quite innocently into the middle of an argument about gunpowder, which ended with one of the parties pointing a gun directly at his chest and firing. The poor salt who had actually been aimed at had run away but the would-be killer, regretful of what had happened, took Avery's body and paid for a nice cart for the burial. Just before he was to be placed on the cart and taken away, he lay alone with a coarse hemp shroud over his face. Avery sat up with a gasp, ripped the shroud off, and sprinted away, heading for water. He finally arrived at the dock, where he crept aboard a merchant trading vessel bound for the Indian Ocean.

A stowaway, hiding in the hold among sacks of pepper and piles of tarnished plate, he'd examined the bullet hole over the course of the voyage and watched it heal itself. He looked up into the starry heavens and (whispering) demanded an explanation. When the ship made berth, he took from the quartermaster's cabin a packet of the finest rat poison, and once he reached land, tipped it into his mouth like a bag of liquorice allsorts. He'd also taken the bosun's cutlass, and he raised it towards himself and—

When Avery finally, fully, realised the truth, he'd set off on a gunpowder-rum-and-firewater bender that lasted for weeks and weeks all the way across Madagascar.

#

The eighteenth century was a blur, and truth be told, he eventually tired of the petty crime and evasion required by his life of smuggling and fraud. Immortality didn't entail drawing attention to your extraordinary self—indeed, quite the opposite was needed, and there was no thrill in it after a while. But, finally, he reasoned that enough time had passed to rejoin society properly under another name, and he criss-crossed the world looking for where and how to do this, until at last he ended up in Europe. A marketplace in Venice would lead to Avery's seventh good day; a drizzly nondescript October afternoon some time in the eighteenth century, when he joined in with a group of poets, artists, musicians, classicists and lawyers-in-training who were enjoying a lengthy Grand Tour of the classical world. Recognising Avery's English accent as he bartered aggressively with a gondolier, they had approached and asked what brought him to the country, and Avery, clocking them as men of means, answered with all due politeness. They fell into friendliness immediately, and the young men explained they were on a gentlemen's educational tour across Europe, of the sort that every serious student of culture must aspire to these days, the very thing for current modern times. They were impressed by Avery's familiarity with tales of adventure from antiquity and soon invited him to join them on their travels. The best day for Avery during this time came when the group visited a sprawling ruin in Rome. He was admiring a small sculpture of Poseidon that stood on a crumbling plinth. At least, perhaps it was Poseidon—a nautical figure, all muscle and a far-flung gaze, standing firmly astride a great stone wave, with one arm raised to throw a spear (or trident) which was sadly missing.

'Does it strike as pleasant to your taste?' one of the group asked him; a playwright and satirist from London who spoke with much enthusiasm about how much he missed the Covent Garden coffee.

Avery professed admiration for the small figure. He liked the way it seemed to have an eye on the distant horizon, watching it narrowing, narrowing, narrowing—

'Well, if you like it, why not take it back with you? The rest of us have all got a souvenir, y'know, Jack. You should have one too.'

At his friend's encouragement, an incredulous Avery pulled the sculpture from its plinth, brushed off the loose stone, and held it out before him. What, he was able to simply take this, right from under the noses of the locals? As he tucked the sculpture under his arm, out of habit his mind began to turn with options, getaway routes, bribery, blackmail, ways to get away with it.

His friend noticed his furrowed brow, and waved away his concerns with a casual hand. 'Everyone who does a Grand Tour gets to enjoy the local beauty, and mementos are encouraged,' he said. 'There's plenty to go around. It's fine. I've got this ancient scroll, look.'

Henry Avery stayed with the group as they travelled on to Naples for the next part of their Tour on the study of music (where he received many compliments on his fiddle technique); after that, he said goodbye, and embarked on his own across the channel to England, and thence onwards to London.

#

Avery enjoyed the nineteenth century, but he did have one truly terrible day in December of 1904, which frankly put him off the whole of the twentieth century just as it was starting. It was the day he attended the world stage premiere of *Peter Pan*.

Not that he was unaware of the increasing romanticisation of his profession. Indeed, nearly two centuries earlier he had proofread an early copy of Daniel Defoe's *King of Pirates, Being an Account of the Famous Enterprises of Captain Avery*, which he had liked very

117

much and had only suggested cosmetic corrections on. In fact, reading Defoe's account of his life would have made the count of his very good days if it hadn't been for how hungover he was at the time. But this was something else entirely. Avery sat in the middle of the front row with a scowl on his face and his arms folded all the way through, and he did not clap at any point, not at the interval, not during the bows, and *absolutely* not when asked to express a belief in fairies.

#

Avery had to wait a while for his next good day. It occurred fairly early on into the twenty-first century, when he resigned from his job on Wall Street.

Not that the position hadn't been great for him. He had to pinch himself sometimes. In the olden days he'd had to plan his treasure heists exceptionally carefully to get even a fraction of what he was getting now, not including the yearly bonus. Plus, back then, the general idea in the world had been to at least keep *rough* track of how much money there was to go around. He'd known plenty of counterfeiters, but they'd had to carefully measure out their materials as much as anyone else. But here, he had been given supreme rule and ultimate dominion over his own private, seemingly infinitely bottomless treasure chest, and he was allowed, nay encouraged, to put in as many doubloons as he liked, and also he was in charge of minting the doubloons, and he could decide how many got made, and how many of those went into the chest, and nobody ever checked. Avery had thrived in the environment. He'd understood immediately the importance of striding across the trading floor as if it were the deck of a swinging ship, the chit papers flying about him like a whirlpool at his heels, and he'd taken to the lingo with all the enthusiasm of his old salt's vocabulary. Then, one day, he'd sensed something; a change in the air, a coming turn in the direction of the wind that just wasn't right. He trusted that shiver on his skin and overnight he'd packed a few things into a cardboard box, wiped all traces of his actions, and left the offices with his desk as blank as his record. And he'd had a feeling in his chest, that this would prove to have been a very good day.

Not too long after that, in a small café somewhere in the south of France, he'd watched on a television screen in the corner as his former colleagues left the same offices, also with a few things in cardboard boxes but with a much more crestfallen attitude, while drastic words of disaster and collapse filled the ticking bar of text along the bottom of the screen. He'd drained his eighth coffee and put the cup down with a sense of achievement keener than anything he'd felt on the trading floor. Yet again he'd sailed off with his treasure haul intact, and as for the rest of the crew—he ordered another coffee with the discreet raise of a finger—well, as for the rest of the crew. They'd let themselves get left behind, it seemed to him, and they could go hang as far as he was concerned.

#

Avery's ninth good day took place fairly recently, when he took a trip to a museum in Edinburgh to see an exhibition entitled *Plunder, Power and Pox: (Re-)figuring Figures of Piracy, 1520-2020*. He wondered how he might be represented (if he were included at all: he braced himself for a bad possibility)—and he was pleased to see phrases such as *King of the Pirates*, *most successful pirate in history*, *legendary plunder never found* and so on, all over the signage; the exhibition also made great show of the mystery of his death which was satisfying, and he enjoyed casting a knowing eye towards his fellow museum-goers when they were reading about it. Nevertheless, he generally preferred Defoe's account of his life. He wasn't at all impressed with the exhibition's sympathy for those aboard the treasure fleet he had captured, or indeed the general fate of anyone who'd encountered him. The tide seemed to be turning on that one.

In a small side-room, Avery made a discovery that put his frustrations with the main exhibition from his mind. The room collected a few artefacts together that were dedicated to ancient masters of the sea, and in a glass cabinet he recognised the statue he had brought over from Rome on his Grand Tour, back in the eighteenth century; so many years ago and there it was, still with one arm drawn back to throw an absent spear, a little more crumbled than before (most of the face was missing), but unmistakably the same statute. He'd wondered what had become of it.

His eye was caught by the sign on the wall, welcoming visitors to the antiquity room. In curling letters was a quote from an ancient captive pirate's response to Alexander the Great. The exchange (as related by Saint Augustine in *De civitate dei 4.4*, so the sign said) went as follows: '...the king asked the man, what had he been thinking, when he infested the sea? To which the pirate replied, with open contempt: "The same as you, when you infested the world; but because I do it with a single ship, I am called a bandit; because you do it with a fleet, you are called an emperor!"'

And Henry Avery had laughed and laughed and laughed. He wished he could go back to be brothers with that pirate. Alas, his life wouldn't stretch to such a miracle. He left the museum whistling a shanty he remembered from the old days, striding with as much purpose as ever along the cobbled streets, that were still shining with recent rain.

#

Keep an eye out; his next good day is today.

# THE CURSE OF THE EMERALD EYE

Cameron Trost

It was shortly after nine o'clock on a Monday morning. The weather was dreary but rather mild for December. Two gendarmes from Guérande had just arrived at the beach in Pen-ar-Ran, not far from the seaside town of Piriac. They were hardly expecting a crowd, but protocol is protocol, and the scene had to be cordoned off.

The short stretch of beach between two craggy outcrops was reached by carefully negotiating a steep flight of concrete stairs. At the top of this staircase, a track led past a glorious but empty holiday house on one side and a less glorious but equally empty 1940s German pillbox on the other before opening onto the street running parallel with the coast. Closing the beach off was simply a matter of blocking access to the track. The gendarmes did this by tying one end of a length of red-and-white tape around the granite corner post of the holiday home's perimeter wall and the other around the trunk of a maritime pine.

The only member of the public already on the beach was the jogger who had discovered the body. She'd called the Gendarmerie Nationale and agreed to stay in place to ensure no one touched the body. Easy enough—in the ten minutes or so it had taken them to arrive, not another living soul approached the top of the stairs—and who in his right mind would go anywhere near the corpse anyway?

The elderly man wearing green pyjamas and a burgundy dressing gown was caught at an atrocious angle on one of the sharp boulders at the bottom of the sea cliff—a good ten-foot drop. His head and arms hung limply on the seaward side of the rock and the lower part of his body hung on the inland side. Death would have been instantaneous, his spine snapping on impact, and the dark streaks reaching down the granite from the back of his head bore witness to

121

the frightful impact that had taken place between bone and stone. Limp like seaweed, he hung there like an offering to some ravenous deity, one unlikely to be satisfied with such a modest morsel. His pale belly stared skyward between green pyjama top and bottom at the highest point, and beneath his slight frame the burgundy dressing gown was splayed out over the natural altar like wings of blood.

'Do you recognise him?' one of the gendarmes asked her.

She shook her head and then said something about it being difficult to know from this angle.

It was the first of many questions, but the gendarmes knew the answers to this dramatic death lay not with the jogger who'd called it in but up there on the private property overlooking the beach.

Identifying the deceased couldn't have been simpler, because as it turned out, he was the owner of the property. The circumstances of his death, however, would remain shrouded in mystery.

The investigators who took charge of the case immediately suspected foul play and hoped forensics would be able to fill in the gaps. They hoped in vain. The time of death was placed at around midnight. The distance from the edge of the cliff made a simple slip seem unlikely but not impossible. Suicide? It didn't seem to fit. Why would a widower of comfortable means who was a leading member of several associations and in considerably good health for his age leave his house in the middle of the night and fling himself backwards off a precipice? Murder? An inspection of the beach and property would turn up nothing of value in terms of evidence, nor would the investigation into his life.

Of course, this isn't a detective story with a mastermind sleuth at hand to solve the puzzle—although you, Dear Reader, may wish to rise to the challenge and answer a question or two before we're done. If it was murder, it was an exceptionally clever crime. There were no tangible clues, no witnesses, and no clear motive or suspects. The authorities were baffled. The public, of course, was happy to speculate wildly. Many of those who believed it was murder—not misadventure or suicide—were also convinced the killer would never be caught. The reason for this belief, however, had nothing to do with the murderer's talents or the ineptitude of the investigators. The being's very nature was what they questioned. A contentious appraisal to say the least, but not one that was entirely baseless.

122

You see, it was later made public that in the days before his death, Gérald Le Berre, leading expert on the history of piracy and privateering in southern Brittany, mentioned to Ludovic Fohanno, his closest friend and a fellow historian, that he was being haunted. In the light of what followed, Monsieur Fohanno expressed the deepest regret for laughing off his friend's claim as a flight of fancy, telling him flippantly that his lifelong obsession had finally taken its toll. Nevertheless, while he wasn't a superstitious man by nature, Monsieur Fohanno refused to accept that his friend had indeed grown mad or suicidal, and so he found himself giving serious thought to the words of these colleagues, neighbours, and complete strangers who pointed out—with inescapable logic—that even the greatest detective in the world could not apprehend the ghost of a fifteenth-century pirate.

#

He recalled that first night in October, he'd not been in bed long when he was roused by a strange voice in the garden. A widower living alone these past seven years and with no children or grandchildren visiting at the moment, *any* voice coming from the garden was bound to be strange, midnight or not, but this one was low and haunting, and the words sounded at odds, somehow both familiar and foreign.

He fumbled for the bedside lamp, put on his glasses, got out of bed, and went over to the bedroom window with its burgundy shutters. He opened the windows but left the shutters closed. He could hear the voice more clearly now, but his hearing not what it once had been, it was still difficult to make out the words. That tone though was unmistakeably sinister, and the way the voice seemed to be repeating the same three words over and over again—not so much speaking but chanting—gave him the shivers. It was not, however, in Gérald Le Berre's nature to tremble behind shutters. He hadn't yet come to believe in ghosts, and he wasn't going to let whoever was mucking about down there get the better of him. He opened the shutters and peered out, knowing what he should see on a moonless night—the dark silhouette of the maritime pine in the left-hand corner of an otherwise bare garden, a sprinkling of stars in the heavens, and in front him, between the stone perimeter wall below and the longest limb of the pine above, nothing at all, except perhaps the navigation lights of a distant ship in the black void of the Mor Braz. What he did see, if he could believe his eyes, he could never have anticipated.

A green orb was spinning in mid-air. It was translucent and glowing, its light seeming to come from within. Where was it precisely? Distance was difficult to judge in the dark. There was no juxtaposition. Without knowing the size of the orb, there was no way of being able to judge how far away it was. At a guess he would say near the wall, beyond which was a narrow smugglers' path—closed to the public for safety reasons—separating his property from the sea cliff. In terms of altitude, roughly halfway between the ground and the level of bedroom window—so that in daylight its backdrop would be the sea, framed by the wall and the pine limb.

He realised the chanting had stopped the moment he'd opened the shutters. He was alone in silence, staring absurdly at that glowing orb—and then it vanished, leaving utter darkness. Steeling his nerves, he donned his dressing gown, left the bedroom, and made his way downstairs, carefully—he'd never know what was going on if he fell and broke his neck. He took the electric torch he kept handy on the kitchen bench in case of blackouts, grabbed a heavy frying pan, and ventured into his back garden.

No chanting. No green orb. Nothing out of the ordinary at all. He peered over the waist-high stone wall and flashed his torch both ways along the smugglers' path. Even though it was officially closed, he'd noticed kids passing along there before. In any case, there was no one to be seen now along the two-foot wide track. He swept the beam of his torch along the dirt track but found no sign anyone had been there. What else was there to do but go back to bed and wait for sleep, though he knew it would drag its heels?

The second time was much the same. He'd been lying in bed, not quite asleep, when he heard the ghostly voice. It was then that he realised he'd been expecting it, knowing without really thinking about it that it was the new moon again. He checked the time on his smartphone—*midnight*. For a month—one full moon cycle—he'd been pondering what he'd witnessed. He had come across no end of strange things over the years, and he had indeed brought to light a good number of mysteries himself—but this was beyond the bizarre. He was going to react differently this time. He wouldn't turn the bedside lamp on, even though he was quite sure it couldn't be seen from outside with the shutters closed, but he would instead make his way carefully downstairs in the dark and try to see the glowing orb from the living room window.

The view from the ground floor offered little more insight. All he could tell was that the emerald orb was in the very same spot as last time. He gritted his teeth and moved to take the iron frying pan and torch from the kitchen. The same three words were being chanted but the chanting stopped when he reached the door to the garden and the orb vanished.

He unlocked the door, swung it open, and peered into the night.

'Damn you!' he hissed more loudly than intended.

He wasn't expecting what happened next. One word reached his ears—one of the three—coming from the smugglers' path, and somehow that haunting voice was low and loud, sounding near and far at the same time. This time, he understood it, and he knew why he hadn't before. He knew why it had sounded both familiar and foreign the first time. It wasn't really either. It certainly wasn't the latter, for it was a Breton word, and therefore belonged to the tongue spoken long before French became *de rigueur* across the land. It was a word he recognised now that he'd heard it clearly, because he'd come across it many times in his research.

'*Mallozh*,' he whispered, still staring into the black night. Empty. Silent. Full of dread. He couldn't close the door fast enough. *Mallozh*. There was no mistaking it. The Breton word for *curse*. The second word fell into place now—*wer*. That's what he'd heard. *The green curse*.

He found himself checking that he'd locked the door, and this reassured him. It meant his mind hadn't left him just yet. His instinct was to protect himself against a physical threat. He told himself he ought to call the police, but he was afraid they would laugh at him and send an ambulance instead.

But that wasn't all, was it? There was another reason.

'Go back to bed, you old fool,' he said aloud without meaning to, and his voice spooked him.

He climbed the stairs and crawled into bed, reminding himself that curses didn't exist and that whatever the green orb was, it couldn't be the Emerald Eye. He'd buried it where no one would ever find it so many years ago. He didn't believe in curses. No reasonable man could. How many times had he told himself that over the past fifty years? He didn't believe in curses—but why then, he always ended up asking himself, had he dug such a deep hole in heavy clay to bury such a precious gem?

#

The December new moon fell on the first day of that darkest of months. It was the third and last time Professor Gérald Le Berre would behold the emerald orb. His sleep had been troubled since the October new moon, and with two months of restless nights, it was hardly surprising that his mind—sharp despite the years—had grown tired and confused. He'd confessed only to his closest friend, but Ludovic Fohanno had failed to take the matter seriously. *A pirate's curse? Good one, my man—a real thigh-slapper! You're not serious? It must be local kids playing a prank. They have amazing gadgets these days—drones and the like.* He'd brushed off Gérald's assurances that it couldn't be a drone, even though there had been no whirring, no dark shape at all. Both times, Gérald had seen an emerald orb—*the eye*—spinning in thin air, glowing softly against the pitch-black night. None of that had convinced his friend. A change of routine had been his only advice. Take more exercise and enjoy a short nap in the afternoon to make up for the fitful nights. If Gérald saw it again in December, he promised to stay with him on the night of the new moon in January—a promise he'd never have to keep.

It was midnight now and Gérald Le Berre heard the haunting voice, but this time, he wasn't in bed—he was ready, lying awake on the living-room couch. He'd been staring at the ceiling, following the dance performed by the firelight from his wood burner. He rushed over to the glazed door and pressed his ear to the cold glass. He could now hear all three words clearly enough to understand. *Mallozh wer* followed a moment later by *marv*. Over and over again.
*Green curse. Death.*
He knew the story of the Emerald Eye better than anyone. Legend

126

had it the jewel was the most prized treasure of Yann Talruz, the notorious pirate. His name would most likely have been forgotten if not for the mysterious fate that befell both him and his emerald. Yann and gem alike disappeared. He wasn't killed at sea, as far as could be told, nor is there any record of him being hanged. He simply vanished without a trace, along with the Emerald Eye. One version of the story gave rise to the legend of the curse, claiming Yann was robbed of it and killed, and that as he died, he put a curse on the emerald—*the green curse*—so that his murderer would suffer a violent death, as would any fool who happened to take the precious stone for his own. Another version, the one that earned the emerald its name, claimed the curse was far older than the pirate himself. According to this legend, the emerald eye had been stolen centuries earlier from the statue of a goddess in a faraway land, and it would remain cursed until the day it was set back in its rightful place in the stone socket. There was always, however, that one constant—any man foolish enough to claim the Emerald Eye would promptly meet a terrible end.

Gérald recalled all this in an instant as he opened the door and rushed outside, heading straight for the glowing orb.

He also recalled that night so very many years ago when he'd broken into the empty country manor not far from La Turballe, risking his reputation, but confident he wouldn't get caught, knowing his preparations had been carried out as thoroughly as his research. The time had been ripe, the manor's sole occupant in hospital, likely for the last time. His research had led him to conclude that the emerald was in there somewhere, that it had in fact stayed in the family, for although the Talruz name had vanished with its most famous bearer, the lineage had remained under other guises. It hadn't all gone to plan that night, though, had it?

Just as Gérald reached the Emerald Eye, it vanished, or rather stopped glowing, for there in the darkness he could swear he still saw it floating in mid air. Then he realised there was a dark form standing on the other side of the stone wall, almost close enough to touch. He could see its outline clearly, because white light filtered through what looked like mist or vapour rose from beneath it.

His lips parted but the name was unspeakable—*Yann Talruz*. How could he ask this apparition whether it was the ghost of that legendary pirate? It was beyond absurd. So he stood there, frozen and speechless, and so did the dark and faceless shadow. Utterly still. Completely silent. It seemed in that instant that this was less plausibly a living person than a centuries-old phantom.

'*Mallozh wer. Marv.*'

'Who are you?' Gérald eventually found the presence of mind to ask.

'I am the ghost of Captain Talruz.'

'You are not!' Gérald hissed. 'You are a living man and the game you're playing is despicable.'

'Do you not believe in curses?'

'I do not.' But the words were spoken out of fear, not conviction. 'Curses aren't real.'

'Perhaps we make them real ourselves. Perhaps we are our own curses. Perhaps we are *each other's.*'

Gérald turned to look at the almost imperceptible emerald hanging in the air. He passed his right hand in a cutting motion through the air above it, palm flat and upturned and shaking a little. He felt something catch on his little finger and the emerald—or whatever it really was—jiggled.

'Why all this?' Gérald asked, his growing dread clear in his voice. 'Why haunt an old man?'

An owl hooted nearby.

'You don't remember? You've pushed it all into the darkest corner of your mind?'

But of course he remembered.

'Who are you?'

'Her grandson,' the shadow growled.

After all these years, the ghosts of the past had caught up with him. The old manor—that crumbling old manor. He'd never forgotten. Those rotten floorboards. He could never forget. The way she'd jumped in excitement, danced with the emerald pinched between forefinger and thumb—and then she was gone. He found her broken and bleeding on the ground-floor tiles. Dead, for all he knew—but he hadn't really known.

'You left her for dead, didn't you?'

There was nothing he could have done, was there? Already dead. Beyond saving. Right? He'd fled the scene. No one would know he'd ever been there.

'How did you find out? That was all so long ago.'

'It was yesterday for you, I'm sure, and it has been my whole life for me. You invoked a curse that day.'

Gérald took a step closer to this shadowy figure, taller and more solid than he had ever been, more like his grandmother. 'I'm so sorry. If I could put it all right, I would.'

'You've had half a century to do that.'

'I'll make it all right by you,' he was pleading now. 'There's something you don't know about who I am and who you are.'

'We are both but ghosts!' The shadow hissed, and the owl glided past as the strong arms shot out and slid under Gérald's armpits.

A wail followed by a thud filled the moonless night and then all was as silent as the deepest abyss.

#

Now, Dear Reader, you have enough pieces of the puzzle to get the picture, but let's make it even clearer.

It wasn't much, the caravan by the marshland, but it was his and it has hidden from sight. No eyes watched him here and no ghosts would trouble him any longer. He carefully cleaned the fog machine and removed the screw hook and fishing line from the fake emerald in the costume turban. He took these items not to the local tip but to the one in Herbignac, a good twenty-minute drive away. He emptied the carton containing the turban into the household waste bin and left the fog machine in the recycling and reconditioning shed for electrical appliances. He then drove straight back to his caravan and lit a fire in the old oil drum he used as a barbecue. It was no seaside holiday home perhaps, but the view he had across the misty marshland on a winter's morning was priceless, and the flames kept him warm. Once the fire was raging, he said goodbye to his old trainers and worn black tracksuit. Hardly the apparel of a fifteenth-century pirate, but they'd done the trick.

He smiled to himself and rubbed his hands together as he raised his gaze from the fire and looked out across the marshland to where a grey heron stalked.

There was one item of evidence he couldn't bear to part with.

Instead, he swore to keep it hidden from all eyes but his own. It was his grandmother's journal. She'd kept a record of it all, the legend of the curse, the research undertaken alongside the young professor who'd encouraged her curiosity even though she wasn't officially a student, the discoveries they had made, and the plan he'd hatched. There was no mention of a love affair with her partner-in-crime. No hint as to the identity of her baby girl's father. Little mention of her at all, in fact, except a line here or there making it clear the child's grandparents took good care of her.

The last entry was from the day before the break-in at the abandoned manor. It marked the end of the journal entries and the beginning of a downward spiral that would span generations. A young mother, obsessed with an ancient curse, missing for days, eventually found by a hunter—dead in an abandoned manor with bits of broken floorboards and a halo of plaster around her. No sign of foul play. No indication that another living soul had been there with her. Her superstitious parents were devastated, convinced she'd unearthed the emerald—though no trace of it was ever found—and suffered the fate promised by the curse. They had hidden all her belongings away; her papers, her books, her journal. But they had kept the curse alive, and the daughter had carried it with her all her troubled life—a dark cloud hanging ever over her.

A good man might have been her salvation, but the one who got her pregnant had been anything but that. Seventeen years and a second son later, her story had ended with a cocktail of vodka and marijuana, a violent domestic, and a furious late-night drive straight into an uncompromising oak.

Had the curse then moved on to take its toll on the brothers? The father was sliding deeper into depression and alcoholism, and the eldest son was hot on his heels, taking every drug he could lay his hands on. Was it the curse that had prompted him to find the journal again after all those years, while digging through cardboard boxes in the garage? He'd been hoping to find objects of value that could be sold for a quick fix. Father would never have noticed in his constant state of drunken numbness. The cartons had held nothing of value though, stuffed only with the relics of ruined lives—junk, old papers and articles, and grandma's journal. The temptation to read it had been too great, as had the urge to share the discovery with his brother.

The unleashing of the truth behind the original tragedy had led to two very different reactions. The older brother had confronted the father and refused to believe his slurred promises that he hadn't known—that he'd never read his mother-in-law's journal. The ensuing fight had ended in a rift that could never be repaired and both men diving deeper into an oblivion of drink and drugs.

The day the older brother could take it no more, he parked his car in the middle of the Saint-Nazaire Bridge at half past five on a busy Friday evening so as to ruin as many people's weekends as humanly possible and sent himself plummeting into the Loire two hundred feet below. The father hadn't lasted much longer, taking his final dive in the filthy couch in his very own living room.

The grey heron took flight and soon became indistinguishable from the cloudy sky.

'*Mallozh*,' he whispered to himself '*Mallozh marv*.'

He shook his head. *No—*

No curses. No ghosts. They aren't real, unless we make them so. The emerald had nothing to do with any of it. This curse had been given life by man, and now, he knew it would bring no more harm, for he had done what should have been done so many years ago.

# LES FEMMES SAUVAGES

## Karen Bayly

Mignonette Belain stood on the beach surveying the vast, darkening sea stretching to the horizon, the setting sun an amber glow behind her. An ill wind blew across the ocean to Half Moon Bay, carrying portents only she recognised. Whispers from the Otherworld meant only for her.

The breeze blew her skirts around her legs and ruffled her dark hair, pulling locks loose from her *chignon du cou* and blowing strands across her face. She narrowed her dark eyes, trying to align her actual vision with the one that earned her the nickname "*la fée*".

Somewhere in the distance, a ship journeyed over choppy waters, yar and deadly, her sails billowing in the wind. The pirate brigantine, La Femme Sauvage, carried a crew of reprobates and a dangerous red-haired captain, a woman whose fiery locks matched the flame of avarice in her belly.

Mignonette called out, daring this woman of incandescent hair and nature to capture and use her as an intermediary between death and unbridled wealth.

Even though the wind dispersed her words, the challenge bolstered her resolve. Ahead lay a journey, a beast, a portal. Ahead lay destiny. Her blood sang. She would not refuse.

#

Captain Jacquotte Delahaye peered at the figure on the beach. The woman stood, hands on her hips as if she were willing the crew to hurry.

Once the water was shallow enough, two of her crew jumped out and dragged the row boat onto the sand.

The woman on the beach strode up, determination in every step. 'I believe you are looking for me. I'm Mignonette "*la fée*" Belain.'

She held out her hands, ready to be bound. The lads obliged, their enthusiasm somewhat tempered by the woman's reputation as a witch.

'That was easy,' said first mate Finn O'Reilly.

'Too easy,' replied Jacquotte. 'We'll keep an eye on this one.'

#

Jacquotte sat astride a wooden chair and leaned her forearms on its top rail, regarding her captive for several minutes with curiosity and a modicum of suspicion.

Calling the woman a captive was debatable, given the bold way she delivered herself into the pirate's keeping. And Miss Belain appeared to harbour no desire to leave. Yet Jacquotte kept her captive's hands bound behind her back for caution's sake.

That Miss Belain squirmed under her gaze amused her. Yet where most captives would wriggle in fear, this one turned the movement into something sensual and seductive. Was this a conscious ploy or unconscious and natural? She suspected the former and smirked.

'I wouldn't do that around my men if I were you, Miss Belain.'

'Untie me, then. I'll not throw myself overboard. And you may call me Mignonette.'

Jacquotte said nothing. A level of formality kept the situation under her control—no need to muddy the water with familiarity. Though civility was the mark of a proper leader, it did not diminish the skullduggery required of a pirate captain.

She reached over and fingered the pendant around the woman's neck. A multi-faceted crystal of an unknown type hung from a fine gold chain. 'Pretty.'

'Thank you. It's yours.' Mignonette lowered her gaze, and a shadow of a smile fluttered across her lips. 'As am I.'

Jacquotte let go of the bauble as if stung. 'Don't play the coquette with me. You waste your time.'

The woman's eyes blazed with challenge. 'Then why so angry, *ma chère*?'

Jacquotte cocked her head. 'You're a perverse creature, aren't you?'

'Says Back From The Dead Red!'

Jacquotte roared with laughter. True. She had faked her death to escape her enemies and pretended to be a boy. But her flaming red hair and feminine features betrayed her, so she gave up the pretence. Nowadays, she chose skirts with jackets tailored for the female form. Her men respected her, or else she ordered keel-hauling until they did. She hadn't needed to kill a man yet.

'Be straight with me, and I'll return the favour, Miss Belain.'

'Then tell me your plan, and I will tell you how to make it work. But first, untie me. My hands are numb.'

Jacquotte grinned. 'All in good time. This is my ship. Only I may make demands.'

She rose and stretched, ignoring the daggers in her captive's eyes.

Without another word, she left the cabin, sniggering at the tirade of abuse that followed her.

#

The rigging creaked and groaned as the ship swayed from side to side like a drunken sailor. Mignonette leaned over the gunwale and vomited. Any resolve she'd experienced back on the beach at Half Moon Bay had faded. No one had mentioned how vile she would feel.

A hand grabbed the neck of her dress and hauled her upright.

'Lean over any further, and we'll be fishing ye out of the briny,' said a gruff Irish-accented voice. 'If the sharks don't get ye first.'

'Leave her be, Finn,' replied a cheerful female voice. 'Best you attend to your duties. That new grommet is green at the gills.'

Jacquotte leaned on the gunwale next to her. 'Don't fret your sweet head, Miss Belain. This slop can churn the guts of old salty dogs, let alone young pups and landlubbers. The ocean is an indiscriminate whore and just as untrustworthy.'

'Call me Mignonette.'

The captain ignored the request and thrust a leather-clad metal flask toward her. 'Have a swig of this.'

'What is it? Rum?'

The pirate captain chortled. 'Brandy. Nothing settles the heaves like it.'

Mignonette took the flask, wiped the neck with her skirt, and sipped. The spirit burned her gullet on the way down, but within seconds of the amber liquid hitting her stomach, a pleasant warmth infused her whole body.

'That's not brandy,' she said.

Jacquotte grinned, and Mignonette could not help but admire the beauty and rakish charm of the captain.

'There may be a few spices known for their medicinal properties added, but brandy it is. You feel better?'

Mignonette nodded.

'Good,' said Jacquotte. 'I want you well for what comes next.'

'Tell me your plans.' She turned to face the captain. 'I know you want me to guide you to some fabulous treasure trove.'

Jacquotte stared out across the undulating waters, her expression as unfathomable as the ocean below. When she spoke, her tone held reverence and an uncharacteristic doubt.

'Aye. In the Sargasso Sea, there's a wreck, a cursed pirate ship, rotting in the implacable sun. It should have sunk years ago, yet something uncanny keeps it afloat.'

'And that is where your treasure lies?'

'Aye. And guarding it, a dead crew and a water wyrm.'

'A sea dragon?' A shiver of excitement ran up Mignonette's spine.

A shadow of a frown darkened Jacquotte's brow. 'You don't seem afeared.'

It was Mignonette's turn to gaze over the wide, dark sea. Vast rafts of seaweed lay to the side and ahead.

'My magic destined me for this.'

Jacquotte patted her shoulder. 'I know.'

The words didn't register for a moment, but then they jolted her from her reverie. She turned back to Jacquotte.

'How did you know?'

But the captain had left, headed aft to the wheel. Mignonette followed her progress, impressed with the deference she elicited from the men as she passed. If only her life had been different. Maybe she, too, could have been a pirate.

Most folks knew that her great-grandfather, Pierre Belain d'Esnambuc, practised piracy in his youth before he became

135

Cardinal Richelieu's champion. That he sired a bastard son with a fée from his Guénouville homeland was a lesser-known fact. Though Belain treasured the boy, Louis, and brought him to the Caribbean, his love did not extend to declaring him his rightful heir. That privilege fell to his nephew.

Louis Belain settled on Saint Kitts and married Mignonette's mixed-race grandmother, inserting a fée lineage into the melting pot of the Caribbean. The blood in her veins was both faery and pirate. To live the lives of both would be a boon.

She sighed and turned her gaze back to the sea. Foolish dreams. Her future lay here in the Sargasso Sea. It had been calling to her for an eternity.

#

Several days passed by with no untoward event disrupting their journey. The weather held calm with a light breeze, and the crew carried out their daily routine with the precision of naval men. Mignonette suspected that many of them were deserters. Or willing captives. Like her.

Captain Jacquotte Delahaye inspired loyalty, but more than that, an aura of predestination surrounded the woman. To follow her was to fulfil your purpose, whatever that may be.

At the moment, the captain focused on the floating beds of seaweed, intent on keeping her ship away from danger. Many a vessel had tangled in the grape-like Sargassum to rot and sink, their crews attempting an escape in row boats, but most dying anyway.

All except the ship the captain sought. Mignonette knew of this ship from her grandmother. The galleon, Esprit d'Or, its hull harbouring caskets of gold and jewels, remained afloat as it rotted, its row boats still lashed to the deck, its crew rotting on deck along with their ship.

Only magic could accomplish such a bane. Only magic could overcome it.

Mignonette "*la fée*" possessed the requisite power.

She leaned against the gunwale, sea sickness vanquished, marvelling at the sea creatures frolicking in the ocean's blue and on the weedy rafts. Turtles, crabs, white marlin, dolphinfish—this was the true magic of this world. She would miss it.

Mignonette closed her eyes and offered silent thanks to the Fates for the privilege of this life. That she believed her next would be as blessed was the only reason she'd embarked on this journey.

A loud cry interrupted her reverie, and she spun around to find a hive of activity and excitement on the deck. She followed the gazes of the men.

Less than ten ship lengths away floated the rotting hulk of the Esprit d'Or.

She garnered from the men's chatter that the wreck appeared out of nowhere as if an unseen fog had lifted. Their glances of suspicion revealed a belief in her unfounded reputation as a witch. But her gift was specific and confined to contacting other worlds. Spell-casting, curses, and necromancy remained as mysterious and frightening to her as they did to the men.

For the first time since boarding La Femme Sauvage, Mignonette feared for her safety.

#

Jacquotte scowled, her hands deft on the wheel. Although tempted to say they'd been sailing for hours, what was happening could not be called sailing. The sails billowed though no breeze blew. A wake spread out behind the ship on a glassy ocean. Yet their position and distance to their destination remained constant.

Finn sidled up to her. 'The men are restless. They blame the witch.'

'The opposite is true. Miss Belain is the one who can get us what we want.'

'Then she'd better get to it before she finds herself kissing the briny blue.'

He nodded at a group of men gathered on the forecastle deck, eyeing the oblivious Miss Belain, who stood near the bowsprit gazing at the wreck ahead.

Jacquotte's scowl deepened. Even from here, she could sense their mistrust and agitation.

'Take the wheel, Finn.'

She strode the ship's length, bounding up the stairs to the foredeck.

Without pausing, she shouted at the men.

'Do you have nothing better to do than gaggle like geese? Pull your fingers out and see to cleaning the deck.'

Snow Pete Williams, a wiry old salt with freakish long white hair, sneered. 'And will ye pull your finger out and cease yer role as lickspittle to the witch?'

Jacquotte spun around, drawing a dagger from the leather holder strapped under her jacket, and leapt forward. She grabbed Pete's hair and pushed the blade against his throat, drawing a line of blood. The other men scattered, and she heard Finn shouting her name.

'Cross me, will you? You're a fool,' she said.

She bested the man in height and murderous will, and his trembling told her he knew it.

'I'm only saying what the men are thinking. I'm doing ye a favour, Captain.'

Finn arrived with two men. 'Yer a mutinous bastard, Pete Williams. We should have thrown ye overboard on the way to Saint Kitts.'

'I mean no harm. I'm only looking out for the men.'

Jacquotte pressed the blade harder, delighting at the blood trickling down the snivelling bilge rat's neck. 'And I don't?'

Snow Pete said nothing, and she snorted in disgust. 'Take the blaggard below and tie him up. I'll consider his fate once we are far from here.'

'Captain,' said Finn as the two men dragged the errant Pete away. 'I must protest. Seal his fate now.'

'No. I'll make no sacrifice in these waters.'

'But—'

'Your captain is wise,' said Mignonette, leaving her position near the bowsprit to join the conversation. 'Though it seems we are not moving, we are. We travel across oceans you cannot see. Waters inhabited by all manner of strange beasts.' She glanced from man to woman. 'Now, you wouldn't want to get their attention, would you?'

She focussed on Jacquotte. 'In a few minutes, the sails will drop. Your crew must row this ship to within one ship's length of the galleon and drop anchor. Then you must walk the rest of the way.'

Jacquotte stared at Mignonette, wondering if the woman played her for a fool. 'So we walk on water?'

Below the foredeck, a group of men had gathered, and a few sniggered.

'There will be no water, only traversable terrain,' Mignonette said. 'And do not bear arms. You tempt fate if you do.'

Finn gave a hollow, bitter laugh. 'She mocks us.'

Jacquotte cupped Mignonette's face with one hand, her eyes boring into the other woman. She grunted and said, 'I don't believe she does. It is why she is here, to guide us through the unknown. For what to us is unfathomable is to her as breath. We will do as she says.'

Mignonette smiled, and despite herself, Jacquotte returned the favour.

#

So far, everything Miss Belain asserted proved true. The anchor hit a rocky outcrop at ten fathoms in an ocean Jacquotte knew to be much deeper. The captive volunteered to leave the ship first, and the captain had no reason to argue. The surface below their feet was neither water nor land but seaweed embedded in some glassy substance. Slippery, but walkable.

The pair were halfway to the wreck before their continued existence convinced the crew they could also walk and not drown.

While they waited for the men to catch up, Jacquotte asked, 'What awaits us?'

But Miss Belain, distracted, stared at the surface beneath her feet, and gasped.

The captain followed her gaze. Something gigantic swam below, its silvery-green scales undulating in the pale light.

'What the devil is that? The wyrm?'

The other woman regained composure and turned to the captain, defiance in her eyes. 'That is my concern. Yours is keeping your crew under control. Follow my commands, and all will be well.'

Jacquotte opened her mouth to insist she commanded this group but realised the truth of Miss Belain's words. She did not have control of this situation, and she hated the fact.

What happened next pleased her less. The crew arrived armed when ordered to remain unarmed, and Finn had brought Snow Pete.

139

'What is he doing here?'

'Better the rat in full view than the one hidden from sight.'

'He's your burden, Finn. I hold you to account for his actions.'

Finn winked and stroked his cutlass.

Jacquotte scowled. 'And as for those...'

'We have a right to defend ourselves,' said Finn.

Although tempted to argue, the captain conceded this battle. There would be others for her to win.

She continued, leading the way, with Miss Belain by her side. 'How does the weaponry affect what you do?'

The other woman shrugged. 'I expected it. It's what men are wont to do. Disobey women.'

'Are you criticising my captainship?'

'*Au contraire.* You, *capitaine*, are a rule unto yourself.'

An eerie silence descended upon them as they drew nearer to the ship. The men ceased their companionable teasing, and a frisson of fear rippled through the group.

Jacquotte stood straighter and stepped into the mouldering hulk. To her surprise, she stood on the upper deck of an intact vessel, its masts reaching into the sky, sails furled, its timber as solid as when it plied the seas. The tang of tar and linseed oil hung in the air. She was about to step back out to verify the illusion when Miss Belain grabbed her forearm,

'Don't bother. What you see is bona fide. This ship spans two realities, each subject to different times.'

'You are a witch! I didn't believe it, but—'

'No, *ma chère*. I do not conjure or curse. All I do is see the world in all its forms. A gift of my faery heritage.'

'Your what?!'

The exclamations of the crew stayed any further discussion. The captain turned and held up a hand.

'Quiet!'

Finn glared at her. 'Are we bewitched?'

'No.' Her mind raced for a tale she could spin that didn't involve fae folk. One that would engender enough dread to keep them wary but not scare them into abandoning the quest. 'We are in the realm of the dead, so mind your tongues lest their ghosts come after you.'

'They will only come after you if you take what is theirs,' said

Miss Belain.

Jacquotte shot her a questioning glance. No one had mentioned any ghostly impediments to claiming the treasure. So, was Miss Belain telling the truth or following her lead?

The other woman winked and continued as if she read Jacquotte's mind. 'And what is theirs is what was on this ship before they captured the treasure you and your captain desire.'

Snow Pete grunted. 'How in hell do we know which is what?'

Miss Belain stared him down. 'You will know. But will you pay heed?'

'He will,' said Jacquotte. 'You all will, for if the ghosts don't get you, I will. We haven't come this far to fail, me hearties, have we?'

Their nods of assent reassured her. Only Snow Pete declined to respond, and his sullen expression tempted her wrath, but now was not the time to punish the wretch. That was a pleasure for another time. She addressed her men.

'I'll tell you, this ship has several decks and a labyrinthine hold. The treasure we seek consists of several chests of gold doubloons and a smaller casket filled with precious gems, including a diamond of rare size and beauty. This gem is what I want the most. This is what will secure our future.'

The gleam of greed in the men's eyes made her grin.

'It could be hidden anywhere. So we will search and only take what we came for. No more and no less. What we find, we bring here, ready to transport to La Femme Sauvage. Now, shake a leg.'

She glanced at Miss Belain, but the woman stared over the ocean, sadness clouding her visage.

'You know that diamond is cursed, *ma chère*?'

'I don't believe in curses. My fate is my own.'

'Fate and curses are not uncommon bedfellows.'

Jacquotte considered this and grunted. 'Then, whatever happens, will happen. I want that diamond. It will procure me an island, and I will establish a pirate republic.'

Miss Belain turned and beamed. 'That you will. No matter the cost. Now, attend to your men. God knows they need watching.'

Jacquotte scowled, but the other woman returned her gaze to the ocean, dismissing any further conversation.

The sun barely moved in the sky, and Mignonette lost all concept of time. The captain and her crew had dragged seven chests of doubloons to the assigned place on deck. But the precious gems eluded their prying eyes.

It didn't surprise Mignonette that the casket of jewels remained undiscovered. The peril associated with the diamond would have forced the Esprit d'Or's crew to hide it well. Yet their efforts had failed and cursed them to eternal unrest. Their ghosts lingered everywhere, hovering around the men, watchful, ready to take action should anyone remove any item belonging to the galleon's crew.

Although neither the men nor Jacquotte could see the ghosts, all sensed their presence. Often, a man had grabbed a gold candlestick or other booty, paled, trembled, and put it back as quickly as he had snatched it up. Mignonette could only guess what they felt—and it must be horrifying to cause men as hardened as these to cower. At least they heeded her warnings.

A cry rose from below. The crew had found the casket.

Mignonette held her breath and waited. Her world glimmered, flicking between the current reality and whence she'd started her journey. The cacophony of excited pirates running up the stairs sounded miles away.

Jacquotte burst onto deck. 'We've found it. We've succeeded!'

'Not yet, *ma chère*. Behold.'

It rose from the ocean in an explosion of sea spray, roaring, its silvery green scales shimmering, its eyes orange fire. A sea dragon, ten times the size of the galleon, its maw large enough to swallow them whole.

Mignonette turned to face the serpent and opened her arms. 'I am here.'

The sea dragon swung its magnificent head toward her and sniffed.

Jacquotte rushed to her aid, cutlass raised. The beast snarled and snapped at her.

'Stay back, Captain,' said Mignonette. 'This is my concern. You take your treasure and go back to your ship.'

'But—'

The serpent raised its head as if to strike.

'Now, Captain!'

Then Mignonette laid a hand on the serpent's neck and sang. The world fell away at once, and with clear eyes and a pure heart, she understood where her journey ended.

#

Jacquotte gawped for only a moment, then set about directing proceedings. Though terrified, the men did not question her and scurried to transport the chests and casket back to their ship.

From her peripheral vision, she saw Mignonette holding the sea dragon in her thrall. The woman insisted she wasn't a witch, but what was this if not witchcraft?

Finally, only Finn remained with her. She nodded at him. 'All accounted for?'

Finn shook his head. 'Snow Pete. Found him dead clutching a silver snuffbox, face frozen in fear, tears of blood on his cheeks.'

'He was warned.' She clapped Finn's shoulder. 'Back to the ship with you. I'll be right behind.'

The man hesitated, his lips forming words that remained unsaid. Instead, he bowed his head and left.

Jacquotte returned her attention to Miss Belain and held her hand out. 'Miss Belain. It's time to go.'

The woman continued singing to the beast.

'Mignonette, please!'

The woman ceased her song and smiled at her. 'At last, you call me by my name.'

'Belain is not your name?'

'It is my family name, but I am not my family.'

Jacquotte knit her brows. 'Explain it to me later. The men are on their way to the ship. Come.'

'No, *ma chère*. My way lies here.' She removed the pendant from her neck and held it out. 'Take this in payment.'

'You owe me nothing. I owe you.'

'Then take it as a memento of our time together.'

'I'm not leaving you here.'

'It is not your choice,' said Mignonette. 'It is mine alone. What I do next will be incomprehensible, but it is new life, not death, that

143

awaits me. Here.'

She threw the pendant, and the instant Jacquotte caught it, the dragon opened its gigantic mouth.

'No!' Jacquotte leapt forward, but with a mere flick of a toe, the dragon pinned her against the mast with the tip of one claw.

Mignonette blew her a kiss. '*Je te reverrai, ma chère.*'

Helpless and heartbroken, she followed Mignonette's departing form as it entered the sea dragon's cavernous maw.

The moment it withdrew its mighty claw, she bolted back to the ship, ignoring the blood soaking into her clothes.

#

Jacquotte leaned back in her chair, stockinged feet on the desk, her skirts draping over her legs and the arms of the chair, her bandaged shoulder resting on a soft cushion. Mignonette's gold necklace with its faceted crystal bauble lay in her free hand.

She held it up to the light, marvelling at how it sparkled and the rainbows it created. She would keep this treasure, and not only as a memento. For one day, its owner might return.

Mignonette lived. Of that, she was certain. From where the wyrm had pinned her, she had an uninterrupted view down its monstrous gullet. And instead of darkness, a bluish light shone. No foetid dragon breath, only a warm waft of meadow flowers. And in the distance, the faint strains of fiddle and pipes.

Mignonette's parting words played in her head. *Je te reverrai, ma chère.*

Jacquotte grinned and fastened the pendant around her neck. 'And I'll see you again, m'dear.'

She knew it in her bones.

# STING OF THE SCHORPIOEN

## DJ Tyrer

A plume of water exploded in a dazzling spray of droplets as the cannonball splashed down a dozen yards short of the Black Swan.

'Faster, you dogs!' shouted the first mate, an evil-looking man named Louis Le Boeuf, better known as Hook for the butcher's hook that was his favoured weapon. 'We must go faster.'

But, the frigate's black sails were already straining as they drove the ship forward, bulging with the wind, and the Dutch frigate remained in dogged pursuit.

Josiah Hawkstone, the captain of the Black Swan, cursed. 'I don't like running,' he snapped at his bosun, Christo. 'I didn't earn myself a legend by sacking Fort Holland only to run from a single Dutch ship, and it not even a man-o'-war.'

'Even the most audacious of men must know when to flee,' the bosun observed, tone even.

'True. This Schorpioen is a swift vessel and they caught us by surprise—and we can neither outmanoeuvre nor outrun it. And, the cowards refuse to be drawn into combat.' He cursed again. 'We have to bring it to battle on our terms, Christo.'

The bosun nodded as another heavy stone ball splashed into the sea, only just missing the Black Swan.

For a moment, Hawkstone stood in silence, eyes uncertain, then he began to stalk about the poop-deck. A man of such violence and cruelty that not only his rivals, but his very crew, feared him as if he were the devil himself. His inevitable response to a threat was to meet it head on, not skulk away.

Then, he halted and slapped his hand down on a capstan. 'The swamps.' He pointed southward. 'Into the swamps.'

Christo nodded and relayed the order to Hook who impressed it upon the crew without a hint of choice.

Hawkstone adjusted the ship's bearing and it raced towards the distant coast.

'Somebody fire a damn shot back in reply,' the captain cursed, the latest shot having only just missed them.

Pigface ran to the nearest swivel-gun and loaded it, then touched off the powder and it puffed off a shot that splintered one of the Dutch vessel's posts. It was nothing more than a pinprick, but the crew set up a cheer at landing a blow against the vessel that had been tormenting them.

Chainshot tore through the rigging in response.

'The sting of the Schorpioen,' murmured Christo.

Hawkstone bellowed at his men, issuing orders, sending them scuttling about, securing flapping ropes. The Black Swan began to zigzag in wide sweeps to avoid further shots, while the dark line of the coast grew ever closer.

'Do you think we can make it?' Hawkstone asked, turning to his bosun.

Christo surveyed the swamp. 'We aren't of shallow draft, but the Schorpioen is a little heavier, giving us a slight advantage. And, we have Marrony Jim.' He glanced towards the tall, heavily-muscled black man who was busy straining to bring a rope under control. 'Jim knows these waters and can guide us.'

Giving a curt nod, Hawkstone said, 'Send him to the prow, and have Pigface join him with a lead to take soundings.' He looked out over his crew. 'And, have a boat ready to lower to tow us. Once we're in amongst the tangle, we can't rely upon the wind.'

Shots flew past the ship, tearing holes through the dense wall of trees that framed the island and concealed a treacherous network of waterways from view as Jim guided them towards the mouth of a river that disgorged a flow of brownish water out some distance into the bright blue of the sea.

The Schorpioen pursued them, only to turn away at the last minute, leaving them to sail into the estuary and, then, veer away into the narrow confines of the swamp.

Captain Hawkstone crowed his victory. 'Damn Dutch haven't the stomach to risk the shallows.'

But, Christo sounded a cautious note, saying, 'They may have been wise not to. We've lowered the longboat, but the oars may become caught in the roots of these trees.'

The captain snorted. 'Without the Schorpioen in close pursuit, we can take our time to extricate them.' He took off his hat and fanned himself. 'We need a safe place to anchor, then send out men to survey the enemy so we can devise a plan.'

Christo shouted out Hawkstone's desire to Jim, who nodded and began giving orders of his own, jabbing his finger at the air to show which direction they should head, whilst Hook prowled the deck behind him, glaring at anyone failing to show sufficient readiness in responding to their guide's commands.

'Here,' Jim shouted after a time, as the Black Swan entered a lagoon with a sandy spit sheltered by the fringe of trees. 'We anchor here. We have deep water and a wide channel to the next river.'

Hawkstone nodded. 'So we can run, if necessary.'

Not that he had any intention of running again.

'Jim, Pigface, Bear, Mantovano, to me.'

The four crewmen came to their master with an alacrity born of fear, the small Neapolitan, full of nervous energy, bringing up the rear.

'I want you men to go with Hook, taking a boat, and see where the Schorpioen is. Do not embroil yourselves with the Dutch,' he gave the Bear, a large man with dark, leathery skin covered in a pelt of hair, a hard look, 'but return and relay all that you learn.'

The men nodded, some more happy than others.

'Well, you heard the captain!' Louis Le Boeuf cried, waving his hook in the direction of the smallest of the ship's boats. 'Let's be moving!'

Each man seized a musket, save for Hook, who took a pistol, and Jim, who favoured a bow fully his height, a weapon quite unwieldy in the confines of the boat, but which many a dead man would testify was more accurate than and just as deadly as any firearm.

'Put your backs into it,' shouted Hook as the others began to row, much of the effort falling to Jim and the Bear, who substantially outsized the other two men.

They didn't follow the channel Jim had identified as leading to the next river, but a narrower one between, and sometimes under, the arching roots of the swamp trees. The splash of the oars caused creatures to swim swiftly away in a froth of white foam. Birds eyed them from dark recesses in the tree trunks and things scuttled along the branches with alarming speed, including crabs that clacked their claws in agitation at their presence, whilst, amongst the Spanish moss that garlanded the trees like the long but straggly beards of old men, the occasional serpent dangled, watching them with a pitiless black gaze that caused the little Neapolitan to quail.

Mantovano loosed a string of curses in his own tongue, mingled with others in English, French and Spanish he'd picked up from other members of the crew. 'This is a bad place—everything here wants to eat us.'

Slapping his arm, he killed a mosquito as if to underline the point. 'Bad place!'

There was a sudden hint of movement amongst the branches ahead and, a moment later, Jim held up his hand and called a halt.

The men grabbed for their muskets, but Jim shook his head.

Ahead of them, and then on other branches to their sides and rear, a motley assortment of dark-skinned men in a mixture of clothing from faded and torn breeches and tunics to simpler outfits created from a variety of materials, appeared. The men were armed mainly with bows—some as large as Jim's, most smaller—as well as a couple of rusted-looking muskets and a variety of hand-weapons from knives and clubs to a sword made by studding a length of wood with sharks' teeth, a lone cutlass and a couple of cut-down boarding pikes.

In a fight, the men looked to have a distinct advantage in numbers that made up for any potential disparity in their weapons.

'Marrons,' breathed Mantovano, crossing himself. Despite sailing with one of them, the Neapolitan's mind was full of tales about how the escapees from slavery and their children indulged in the eating of human flesh and delighted in torture, and quivered just a little more than usual at the sight of them. That they had heard comparable tales of the pirates never entered his mind.

The men looked down at them with wide, bright smiles that mocked their discomfort, then Jim spoke, the words strange and incomprehensible to his colleagues, despite snatches of what sounded like Spanish, French, Dutch and, even, English amongst them.

The men lowered their weapons a fraction, no longer immediately threatening, yet far from welcoming. The pirates looked back, nervously.

'Well?' demanded Hook, the fierceness of his voice underlaid by just the slightest tremor. 'Are they friendly?'

Jim laughed, and the bark didn't sound too friendly, while the Marrons continued to grin down at them in a way that, too, seemed lacking in friendship.

He shook his head. 'No, not friendly, no. They hate pale men like you. But, I have vouched that you are not enemies intending to do them harm and have told them of the Dutch, who may. So, as long as I am with you, you are safe. But, never welcome. You understand?'

Hook swallowed and nodded. Pigface and Mantovano did likewise, but the Bear continued to glare up at the men, giving no indication whether he understood or not. Probably, he didn't care either way.

Jim spoke again in the language of the Marrons, then said, 'They will let us pass.'

With that, the men seemed to step back into the shadows cast by the dense canopy of leaves and vanish.

'Like ghosts,' muttered Pigface.

'Like devils,' said Mantovano, crossing himself.

'We proceed ahead,' Jim told them, ignoring their comments, and they resumed rowing, certain they could feel the eyes of the hidden men watching them and the points of their arrows pricking at them from the darkness.

Mud dirtied the water as they went, creating swirling patterns about their oars, as they passed through shallower channels where silt gathered itself about the stilt-like roots of the trees, whilst hanging moss brushed damply against their faces, its touch managing to be both soothing and repellent against their hot, sweaty brows. Mosquitoes hovered about them, producing a constant soft drone, second only to their bites in annoyance.

After a time, Jim raised his hand, again, and called a halt.

He stood and tossed a rope up at a branch, throwing it about it three times before tying a knot to secure the boat in place.

'We are near the sea,' he said. 'Mantovano and I shall go on through the branches of the trees—it is easier to hide two men up amongst the moss than a boat upon the water.'

The Neapolitan groaned. 'Why me? Whatever did I do?'

'Certainly not a day's labour,' chuckled Pigface.

'You're a rigging rat.' Hook paused to spit into the water. 'You climb better than you walk. That is why.'

Crossing himself, Mantovano nodded, but continued to look unhappy at his role.

The boat rocked a little as Jim pulled himself up onto one of the sturdier branches.

With a sigh, but imparting less motion to the boat, Mantovano scuttled up after him.

Pigface and the Bear grasped their muskets tightly, Hook stroking his weapon of choice like it was a talisman, their eyes darting about them at the shadows, hoping Jim's truce would hold firm.

Although a little less adroit at scrambling through the rigging than the Neapolitan, Jim moved through the intertwined trees with ease, his bow slung over his shoulder and less awkward than the musket Mantovano carried in his arms.

Leaves rustled as they crouched in the crook of a particularly broad branch, just within the green screen of foliage. From here, they could observe, unseen, the slow approach of the Schorpioen as it moved majestically along the coast seeking its prey.

There was an explosion of spray as the ship finally slowed to a halt and dropped anchor.

Jim nodded. 'So begins the waiting game. They watch both river mouths for us to leave the safety of the swamp.'

Lacking a telescope, he held a hand above his eyes to shield them from the sun and used the fingers of the other to judge distances and angles with a skill derived from long practice.

He nodded, again. 'I have their position.'

Beside him, the Neapolitan had gone rigid. Jim turned to observe him and laughed. A creature had scuttled out of the recesses of the tree's trunk and was probing carefully along the length of the man's raggedy sleeve, tail arched provocatively over its back.

'So, my friend, you have found a scorpion of your very own. Do not worry overmuch—large ones such as this are far less poisonous than the little ones. Besides,' he added after the briefest of pauses, 'I doubt it seeks trouble for, see, she carries her children upon her back.

150

'Just like the Dutchmen upon their ship!' He laughed, again. 'Oh, move your arm.'

Slowly, wincing as he did so, the Neapolitan obeyed him.

With a wide grin, Jim nodded past him, towards a higher branch and said, 'If you must worry—worry about the serpent above you.'

Mantovano gave a squeal and slithered down to a lower branch, where he crouched awkwardly, while glaring up at Jim.

'Can we go, now—please!'

'Certainly, my friend.' Jim shinned down to join him. 'Follow me.'

#

'The plan is simple,' announced Captain Hawkstone upon their return. 'The Dutch have prepared an ambush for us, ready to strike wherever we emerge, and I will not skulk here in this swamp awaiting their departure.'

He slammed his hand down upon the rail. 'I am no coward!'

Pausing for a moment to slow his breathing, the captain continued: 'If they wish us to emerge, then that is precisely what we shall give them.'

Hawkstone's lips parted in a grin reminiscent of a cat about to pounce upon a mouse. 'Oh, but we shall give them more. We shall give them more than that.'

He looked at Jim. 'Could you guide a longboat through the swamp to the coast where they lie at anchor?'

Jim nodded. 'Aye. I believe so.'

'Good. You will take the second longboat, with muffled oars, and row out to the Dutch ship. At the appointed time, you shall board them. At the same moment, we shall set sail out to meet them. That,' Hawkstone continued, 'should prove sufficient distraction for you to slip aboard.'

'Catching them between two prongs,' grunted Pigface.

The captain nodded. 'Precisely. And, this is how we shall proceed...'

#

It was a plan both simple and easily disrupted, just as it was one of elegance and brutality, and the men who joined them in the longboat were silent less out of respect to the captain's orders, or fear of the first mate's butcher's hook, and more due to a wary acknowledgement of the risks facing them. Likewise, their expressions were dour and there was a certain twitchiness on the part of the more nervous members of the party.

Marrony Jim was at the prow of the longboat with a bullseye lantern, picking out their route through the treacherous tangle of trees, relaying their course by means of barely-visible gestures to Mantovano at the tiller.

Hook was seated in the middle of the men, making certain each one pulled with all his strength to propel them forwards, working the oars, which had been wrapped in canvas to reduce the sound they made cutting through the water.

The battle, when it came, would be a vicious one and both reaching the ship and climbing aboard undetected would be difficult, but actually traversing the swamp was the biggest risk of all: Becoming snagged on or punctured by the trees' roots, being attacked by one of the crocodiles, sharks or other vicious creatures that lurked in the brackish waters, or even being ambushed by Marrons were all potential ways in which their escapade might be brought to a premature end.

Even Jim was leery of the last, acknowledging that a larger party might not be overlooked in the manner of their earlier encounter.

'No matter what we meet,' he told the nervous men behind him in a low voice, 'do not fire your muskets, unless I say to. For, while the trees may muffle the sound, we will likely alert the Dutch to our approach.'

As if prescient, mere moments after lapsing back into silence, an arrow whistled softly out of the darkness and landed with a thud in the side of the boat. Muskets and boarding pikes were raised in response, but no one fired.

Another whistle was followed by a pained gasp of surprise and one of the pirates fell overboard with a loud splash.

Thrusting the lantern into the hands of Pigface, Jim grabbed up his bow, while directing the man where to point the lantern's beam.

Raising his bow, with some difficulty in the confined space, he let an arrow fly and there was a sharp sound of pain, followed by that of hasty and unconcealed movement through the branches.

The boat drifted on in silence for several heartbeats, while Jim notched another arrow, but there were no further attacks.

Jim laid down his bow to resume his duty as guide. As Pigface handed back the lantern, he caught the troubled expression upon the man's face and said a silent prayer of thanks he'd stuck by them.

Reaching the edge of the swamp, Jim doused the lantern and allowed the boat to drift silently out of the swamp's confines into the open sea. Ahead of them half-a-mile, they could see the dark shape of the Schorpioen, hung with lanterns against the darkness of the night.

Checking the stars to reassure himself of the time, Hook gave the whispered order for the men to resume rowing.

With a steady glide, the boat approached the ship across the open water and, backs bent to the oars, every man was filled with trepidation lest the crew of the Schorpioen notice the black shape approaching or catch the soft sound of an oar, the sweat running down them as much from that as exertion.

In the distance, the Black Swan was returning to the sea, ensuring attention was anywhere but upon them.

They didn't have long to act.

Most watchful of all was Jim, crouched in the prow, bow ready to shoot any Dutchman unlucky enough to spy their approach.

But, none did, and they drew up close to the rear of the frigate, keeping some distance away.

The greatest risk was over, but they still had to get aboard.

Jim, Hook and the Bear all stood and lifted ropes attached to grappling irons. There was a distinct whooshing sound as they swung them in arcs above their heads and, then, they released them to shoot up and catch upon the ship's rails.

Now, they allowed the boat to draw in closer to the ship, men reaching out their hands to its tarred hull to prevent the boat from bumping noisily against it.

Men began to climb. Mantovano, silently cursing his luck, was one of the first, shinning his way up the rope with ease. There was a hubbub aboard the ship, but, unless the stars had cursed them, it was due solely to the approach of Hawkstone aboard the Black Swan.

The plan, now, was twofold. Pigface, who possessed some skill with fuses, was to descend to the ship's magazine and set it to blow, while Hook would lead a surprise attack on the ship's crew, before making a fighting withdrawal. Even if the plan proved a failure, they would sow confusion and cause casualties before Hawkstone launched his own attack. And, if it were a success, the Schorpioen would sting itself to death.

'With me,' Pigface told Mantovano, who felt as if he had nothing but ill luck this night.

Keeping low, the pair scuttled over to an open hatch and, quickly, but quietly, slipped down the ladder to the deck below.

But, before they could proceed any further, a crewman stepped out of the shadows and stopped in mid-stride, staring at them in surprise.

They stared back.

Then, before either man could act, the sailor lunged at Pigface and thrust a marlinespike at him.

The pirate attempted to twist away from the blow, but it plunged into the top of his leg and Pigface squealed.

Mantovano swung his musket as a club and landed a blow against the side of the man's head. The sailor gave him a puzzled look and sank to his knees.

The Neapolitan didn't pause, but brought the butt of his musket straight down on the man's head, cracking it open like an egg with a bloody yolk.

He looked at Pigface, who shook his head, hand upon the handle of the marlinespike, uncertain whether to withdraw it.

'I can't walk,' he said. 'You'll have to do it.'

He thrust the fuse and tinderbox at him. 'Make the fuse twelve inches and it should be fine.'

Mantovano muttered some curses of his own invention, but nodded. Hook would skewer him worse than Pigface was, if he just turned tail without even trying.

Leaving his colleague to pull himself back up the ladder, the Neapolitan set off deeper into the interior of the ship.

Sounds of conflict echoed down after him—the loud bangs of muskets and pistols, the clash of steel, the shrieks, cries and groans of dying men being sliced down by cutlasses or impaled by boarding pikes or the first mate's hook. From below, those Dutchmen not required to man the guns against the approaching pirate ship were rushing up to repel boarders, but Mantovano managed to evade them.

The magazine! Unfortunately, a marine in a finely-starched uniform stood guard at its door, musket held ready to his chest.

Montovano half-turned, really wanting to go.

*I did my best,* he thought. *It wasn't even my job, not really.* But, it was, now, and he had to try.

Concealing himself in the shadows, he raised his musket and took aim, the guard oblivious to his presence.

He pulled the trigger and there was a bright, blinding flash and a thunderclap of sound and, when he managed to blink his vision back, a moment later, the guard lay slumped against the door, dead, blood splashed across the white of his shirt.

A little gingerly, Mantovano approached and dragged the dead man aside. The door was unlocked, ready for the battle, and he had no trouble getting inside.

He had only just begun to lay out the fuse when he heard the sound of footsteps on the stairs outside. Swearing, he grabbed his musket, then realised he hadn't paused to reload. Stepping up to the door, he heard a gasp outside—the marine's corpse was clearly visible from the stairs.

Mantovano swung the door open and lunged through it, swinging his musket as a club. Missing the man on the stairs, he didn't have time to dodge as he raised a pistol and fired. Air exploded from the Neapolitan's lungs in a roar of pain as he felt the pistol-ball tear through his liver. Swinging again, he managed to catch the man's legs, knocking them out from under him.

Mantovano fell on the man, more from failing strength than tactics, and managed to tug the knife free from his belt and plunge it into the sailor's guts—once, twice, thrice. The man fell still under him.

Somewhere above him, very far away, Mantovano thought he caught the sound of Hook's voice ordering a retreat—he had to hurry. With difficulty, using his musket as a crutch, he managed to stand and stumble back to the magazine.

He blinked, hardly able to see. No time to do it properly, he tugged out a length of fuse and attached it to a barrel of gunpowder just inside the magazine door.

Where was the tinderbox? No time to search, nor think, he laid the lock of his empty musket beside the fuse and pulled the trigger. A spark, but no luck. With difficulty, he drew the lock back, again, then pulled the trigger. Success! The fuse burst into life.

Desperately, barely able to stand, let alone walk, Mantovano headed for the stairs, groping almost blindly for them and dragging himself up.

Nearby, there was the splintering of wood as a cannonball tore into the hull of the Schorpioen.

He wasn't going to make it.

He really hoped they raised a mug of rum to him.

#

Jim laid Pigface in the bottom of the boat, then paused to bandage a gash in his own arm.

With only one man dead and a few light wounds, the pirates were shinning back down the ropes to their boat to withdraw as the Black Swan drew near.

'Did you do it?' Hook demanded as he dropped onto the boat beside Pigface.

The man shook his head and waved at the marlinespike still embedded in his leg.

'Sent Mantovano.'

Hook gave the impression of being unimpressed by the mention of the Neapolitan's name.

With all the survivors aboard, he gave the order to cut the ropes.

'What about Mantovano?' asked Jim.

Snorting, Hook said, 'He has the time it takes to swing an axe—'

There was a pregnant pause as three men, axes in hand, waited, then they swung them, severing the ropes that had bound them to the frigate.

'Row, you dogs!' Hook waved his namesake to emphasize the point.

Jim grimaced. 'But, Mantovano—?'

'If he set the fuse,' groaned Pigface, 'we'd best be away.'

'And, if he didn't,' finished Hook, 'we must go, regardless.'

Then, as if to clarify the point, there was a sudden, terrible crack of thunder and flash of lightning from within the bowels of the

Schorpioen, tearing through the frigate and setting it afire.

Men threw themselves from it, some ablaze, seeking a dubious sanctuary in the sea, and the Black Swan kept up its fire, ensuring that the wreck slid swiftly below the waves, extinguishing the flames and returning the night to darkness.

A cheer went up from boat and ship at the pirates' victory, but Pigface was unable to issue a cry and that of Marrony Jim was muted. The two men exchanged a silent look, a shared thought for the comrade who had perished aboard the frigate, sacrificing himself for them to ensure the Schorpioen died by its own sting.

#

Smoke rose to greet the dawn, as the men gathered upon the beach to roast boar in celebration of their victory.

'Raise a mug in triumph,' called Hawkstone to his crew, 'and drink a toast to the man who destroyed that Dutch frigate.'

'Mantovano! Mantovano!'

The captain gave a nod of satisfaction. 'Now, feast. But, prepare yourselves—we still have a score to settle and can count on the Dutch to return.'

The men roared their defiance, then they began to eat.

# BEHOLDEN TO NO ONE

## Karen Keeley

I knew nothing of the sea having lived and worked in Shanghai for the better part of three years, appointed secretary to one Leonidas Havisham in May 189—, overseer with a mercantile shipping firm headquartered in the British concession. The investors, all wealthy men with impeccable pedigrees, capitalized on the procurement of oriental silk, porcelain and tea—three of the most sought-after commodities in Britain, coveted as they were by ladies of every station, both high-born and low. The goods, imported from central China were sent by ship to the port of New Romney, seventy miles southeast from London's Royal Docks, a voyage which took anywhere from three to four months depending on the time of year, and sailing conditions.

To awaken and have found myself lying on the deck of the Leviathan made no sense at all. I sat up, the vessel heaving to 'n fro on the great swells, first lifted high upon one wave and then rolling forth, the bowsprit under water only to surface like the great white whale, or so it seemed, and there I was, in the valley of death with nothing but water on either side. I too rolled with the ship, tumbled forward and backward, and how it came to pass that I was not tossed overboard, I do not know but for the fact one leg was tied with rope, the binding securely knotted to my left ankle, the other end tied to what I would later come to learn was the mainsail mast, fore-and-aft rigged for the beating it was taking.

The helmsman, unknown to me at the time, was a buccaneer by the name of Captain Jacques Soho. He stood defiant upon the quarterdeck, his ship plying the waters between the Yellow and the East China seas, a reprehensible rogue known to have plundered loot from all and sundry, the Leviathan's cannons ever at the ready. Its crew, cut-throats all, were adept at swinging a razor-sharp cutlass or firing a flintlock, individuals who neither gave a pittance nor a farthing to matters of life and death. They simply existed, as men do, with hearts blackened by greed, thinking whatever another had, they would take.

As for me, I dearly relished my life for I had a young family in Shanghai in addition to many business associates. I meant to return home come hell or high water, of which I was now experiencing both, my stomach heaving with the rolls of the ship as I hung on with determined resolve, my arms wrapped around the mainmast, the ship tossed about like flotsam and jetsam, unable to make sense as to the how, or the why of it which had placed me in such dire straits, obviously shanghaied. Out of Shanghai, no less, which seemed a bitter irony indeed.

#

'You be brought on board to teach me the fine art of penmanship,' said Captain Jacques the morning after, the seas calmer, the winds abated, me having finally found my sea legs. I'd been released from my tether some hours earlier whereby no one would offer up one word of explanation, nothing but grunts followed by a cuff to the side of the head which left my ears ringing and my vision blurred.

Captain Jacques continued, 'I be a seafaring man since a wee babe, never properly taught the A, B, Cs. Oh aye, I be good with the rudimentary elements of the craft, but I now be desiring to know the finer aspects. You be teaching me that.'

I stood, dumbfounded, remembering yesterday's ordeal, tossed about on deck like a captured seal pup, clubbed by the wind and the waves, then shoved into some forward cabin, the door securely locked, this morning's bowl of foul-tasting fish stew flung at me along with a meagre slice of stale bread, both meant as compensation for the pain I had endured.

I choked it down, knowing the need to keep up my strength if I were to ever make it home again, reflecting on the why? Had I been kidnapped for ransom, and if so, would my employer pay the price, for my wife and I certainly had no money with which to secure my release. Me, nothing more than a secretary known for my fine penmanship.

I surmised I must have been accosted whilst making my way through the port area of Shanghai, enjoying the sights of the mercantile sailing ships, listening to the banter amongst the seamen as they scurried about, climbing the rigging and swabbing the decks, others heartily singing sea shanty songs. I'd walked that stretch of the city many a night, inhaling the briny air, with nary a single individual taking notice of me, the memory of my attack gone, taken aboard this vessel, no one the wiser but for those who committed the foul deed.

Presently, after the so-called meal, I was taken to the captain's cabin, and there he sat, speaking of the desire to learn the finer points with regard to the Queen's English, all of which I deemed utterly preposterous.

I stared at him, anger rising within. 'I'll do no such thing,' I stated. 'I mean for you to return me to dry land immediately. I will then venture forth, more than content to be rid of the lot of you, nothing but heathens and scoundrels—murderers, too. To that end, I am willing to forget this most unpleasant ordeal has occurred, to simply put it behind me.'

Captain Jacques leaned back in his chair, much like that found within the halls of business with its oak construction and polished armrests, the chair on casters, and he roared with laughter. 'A man after my own conviction,' he bellowed. 'Such bluster and bother, a bedeviled sight for sore eyes. Your clothes be in ruin, you, yourself, in badly need of a shave.' His eyes grew hard, mean as a jungle predator seeking its next prey. 'How dare you be speaking to me in such a tone. I could have you whipped for such insolence.'

'Whipped, you say! In this day and age? Not at all a gentlemanly act.'

Again, he roared with laughter. 'It be my uncle who gave me my name, telling me I was destined for fame, or infamy, or both. Do I look the gentleman to you?'

'You look a scoundrel and a thief, just as I have said, and a kidnapper. To have removed me from my place of employment and family, that sir, is beyond reprehensible.'

'Family, you say. How about this? You be doing what I ask and I'll not be bothering your family. You disobey me, and I'll be tossing

160

you to the fishes. Following that, I will seek out your fine pretty wife, and make sport of her!' He slapped his knee as though that revelation just occurred to him, but I again saw the cruelty in his eyes, confirming he was capable of such terrors, his victims tormented, their very souls crying out for release.

The blood ran cold in my veins. 'The fine art of penmanship, you say.'

I now regarded this devil of the high seas in a different light, one not to be intimidated, and certainly not by me. He was an appalling individual, bandy-legged, barrel-chested, one who reeked of barnacles and rotted fish, his attire something dredged from the deepest depths.

'Ah, good man. I see we've struck a bargain. I will be offering you a good portion of my time and you will be teaching me the finer points required. When not so doing, you shall have the freedom to wander the ship and do as you please.' He shouted for Cook, the man who'd locked me in my cabin. 'You be taking Mister—,' he paused and scratched his chin, his long-plaited beard threaded with beads, his wild tangled locks of ginger hair flecked with grey, truly confirming his look of a madman. 'It behooves me your name, having not been properly introduced. I am Captain Jacques Soho, master of this fine vessel, the Leviathan, and you are?'

I told him, sneering my name as though it were a cursed thing. 'Rupert Bartholomew Rey, spelled R-e-y, not your typical r-a-y.'

His eyes narrowed. 'Do you mock me? If so, you shall forthwith join the fishes!' He just as quickly softened his stance; his anger abated. 'But no, never mind. Cooky, you be seeing this beleaguered guttersnipe is supplied with decent clothing whilst his own be drying out in the galley.'

Cook grabbed my shoulder and spun me about. Captain Jacques addressed me one final time.

'Welcome aboard, Rupert Bartholomew Rey. Henceforth, you be known as Moggy, the look of a drowned cat about you, small in stature but aye, such bravado! Something to be admired.'

And thus began my ordeal aboard the pirate ship, the Leviathan. Small in stature and big in personality, myself and the ship. As to why Captain Jacques needed to acquire the fine art of penmanship, I had yet to learn.

161

Some time later, my clothes taken from me and set to dry properly in the galley, then returned to me, I found that I too reeked of barnacles and rotted fish, the very stench of it all ingrained into my pores. As to that state, no one noticed nor gave a farthing's worth of concern.

I was brought before Captain Jacques, whereby I told him, 'For a man who claims he can neither read nor write, you do have the way of a learned gentleman about you,' taking note of his cabin, luxurious in its finery, satin bedding, silver candelabras, exquisite Chinese porcelain upon his table, and oriental works of art hung upon the walls, dragons and cherry blossoms.

He laughed uproariously, and slapped his knee. 'Me thinks you be mocking me once more, but I be leaving that for now. I will tell you, prior to your arrival, I enjoyed the company of various men of distinction brought aboard. Some remained with us but a few weeks, others a few months. I mimicked their speech, their mannerisms, a theatrical enterprise on my part.'

'To what purpose?'

'Why, entertainment, of course.' A man most callous, this captain of the Leviathan, a fine oak vessel capable of eleven knots, its weight somewhere in the region of one-hundred tonnage, its crew of twenty, the captain obviously playing a game of cat and mouse with those shanghaied into service, and now my turn for the taking. 'A distraction, an interruption to break up the monotony whilst at sea,' he said. 'It did not occur to me to avail myself of their knowledge, to have one of them teach me the craft of which I desire. But now, I be having need of that, thus your presence amongst us.'

'Your advantage and my folly,' I told him, thinking of my dear spouse, and her having no knowledge as to my whereabouts, believing me likely dead. And what of my employer? Worry would have been paramount in both their hearts, ignorant as to my welfare.

'Shall we leave it there?' he said. 'Tomorrow, we begin the lessons. You will find I be a quick study. If you be any teacher worth his salt, the sooner you be teaching me, the sooner you be put ashore to make your way homeward bound.'

A quick study. I hung onto that, thinking if I were to be nothing more than a distraction, something to relieve his boredom, I too could play the game.

Thus, the lessons began whilst I endeavored to make sense of the man who now took on the look of a British Admiral in the Queen's navy, more officer than pirate, with his silk trousers and stockings, silver buckled shoes, a ruffled shirt, his clothes flamboyant in their colour and cut. An hour into his studies, he noticed candle wax on the cuff of one sleeve and was most put out with himself. He changed into a clean garment, his muscles rippling, not an ounce of fat on him, his grip surely that of an iron vice, capable of squeezing a man's throat in a single heartbeat. Once newly attired, he then toyed with a gold filigree pocket watch hung on a chain, handling the timepiece in an almost delicate manner, as if time itself were running out, and he with it.

At first, he had me read newspaper articles to him, the broadsheets plundered during his travels which gave him great pleasure, especially those stories with regard to piracy. He most notably enjoyed the ballads written on newsprint and sold for a penny a piece in the streets of London. The fact that many a commoner took great delight in the age of pirates, much caught up in the idea of democracy, shared labour and shared loot, swayed public opinion in favour of the cut-throats, their plunders to be cheered and sung about.

Within a week, Captain Jacques' reading level had elevated to that of a child of nine or ten, his finger following the words as he attempted to sound out the word phonetically. I encouraged him where I could, withstood his foul language when he berated himself, sat at his table during meals, of which he hardly ate, perhaps struggling with his desire to master the finer art of penmanship, and me, livid at my confinement.

'This through and threw, it makes no sense!' he cried, and I agreed. Contractions too drove him mad, as did prepositions. I tried to explain the idea of a log—at the log, about the log, over the log, of which he thought was the most ridiculous thing he'd ever heard.

'That may be,' I told him. 'But it makes a mental picture.'

When he was tired, his speech floundered, often slurred, words misspoken. I made no comment, not wanting to feel the wrath of the back of his hand. 'I do not be needing a mental picture; I need knowledge!' he shouted.

'Reading comes from seeing the word as a whole, not divining individual letters.'

'You be explaining,' he said, so I did.

To my surprise, his library was extensive: books, periodicals and maps taken during raids. A complete copy of the Koran in its original Arabic. Collected works of Chaucer, Shakespeare, Lord Byron, and more recently, the writings of Oscar Wilde, telling me Wilde's epigrams of a satirical nature were most entertaining.

'And you know this how?' I'd asked.

'Some of those on board prior to your arrival, I had them read to me. Most illuminating.'

There then came a day, he showed me his most coveted prize, a handwritten scroll, that of the Jewish Torah, containing the five books of Moses purported to be thousands of years old. How many lives traded to attain such a document, I dared not ask.

As to buried treasure, another day when he'd tired of the reading, his eyes strained, a headache coming on, he leaned back in his chair, pointed, and bid me to discover for myself that which he had plundered, treasure stored in a large wooden chest, it having been placed under the span of windows at the aft of the ship with a sternway balcony attached, the chest covered by a linen tablecloth, hidden in shadow.

I removed the tablecloth, struggling to lift the lid on the chest, the weight of it very much like wrestling with the weight of a large wooden barrel, eventually throwing back the lid where it banged the ship's planking. To my utmost astonishment, I discovered gold doubloons, silver coins, jewels by the boatload, silks and tapestries, chalices and candlesticks, the chest full to the brim. As to its worth, I couldn't begin to imagine, but I had heard stories whereby some pirates had looted treasure worth a King's ransom which truly staggered the mind.

#

As to the running of the ship, all crew had their duties and heaved ho. I came to learn the layout: the bowsprit, the stem, the foc's'le, and

164

the mainmast. I was allowed on the quarterdeck when O'Grady was at the helm, or I simply kept company with Cook in the galley, helping him much as a scullery maid would do, peeling potatoes, chopping onions, when relieved of my duties with the captain. As for the sails, there were many: the main royal, the topsail, the fore royal, and toward the stern of the vessel, the mizzen royal and spanker, all of it Greek to me, a language unto itself.

Many an evening I stood on deck at sunset, the ship rising and falling with the swell of the ocean as I watched the giant ball of our sun slipping beneath the waves, painting the ocean into vibrant hues of silver and gold, amber highlights upon the foam. Seabirds flew high in the distance, diving for fish, possibly a shoal of herring near the surface, those small fish darting to 'n fro, some seeking protection in the centre of the shoal, others on the outer ring exposed to attacks from above, possibly barracuda or mackerel in the deeps, they too feeding. I then approached O'Grady, the helmsman, he on the quarterdeck, and mentioned in passing, 'I do not understand my role in all this, teaching the captain to read and write.'

O'Grady laughed heartily, throwing back his massive head, his blond locks tangled by the wind, a mischievous glint in his eyes. 'The captain! Why, he be a master at readin' and writin' same as the rest of us, how else do we be doing the navigating with the maps? As for the captain, he be the keeper of the ship's journal, and the logbook, when he has a mind to.'

That comment threw my thoughts into turmoil. 'But each day, I spend hours with him, slowly going through the alphabet, him trying to make sense of it all.'

'He be toying with you,' said O'Grady. 'It be common knowledge amongst the lot of us, he be the one to dangle the likes of you on a string, make you dance like a wooden puppet.'

The cheek of the man! Kidnapping me, bringing me aboard the Leviathan, separating me from my dearest loved ones. 'I'll have his head on a platter,' I mumbled, knowing instinctively the outcome of such an endeavor, my head on a platter, a fool's errand if there ever was one.

Again, O'Grady laughed heartily. 'You try such a thing; you be fed to the fishes.'

So there we were, my role to be that of entertainer, someone to be trifled with. What possible outcome was expected, I had no answer. I took myself to bed.

On another night, O'Grady shared a terrible story whilst he steered the ship, a south-southwest wind moving us forward, foam plying the sides of the Leviathan, the waves looking as quicksilver in the moonlight. 'There was a time one of our crew came aboard with a headful of lice, a terrible affliction. We be anchored in a wee cove on the leeward shores of Rodrigues Island, cavorting with the locals, making merry with whisky and rum, much revelry to be had. You've heard tell of the place?'

I nodded, one of many islands located in the Indian Ocean offering sanctuary to pirates and cut-throats seeking to escape the law.

'We threw the vermin overboard—'

'The lice?' I inquired.

O'Grady laughed from his belly whilst giving me a hearty slap on my shoulder. 'No, me bucko. The man. We had a devil of a time ridding ourselves of the vermin, all of us picking nits out of our scalps and beards for weeks.'

'And what of your shipmate?' I asked.

'He be shark food, and us the better for it.'

That night I suffered nightmares, many legged insects the size of rats scurrying about the upper decks, making their way en masse through to the fo'c'sle and the hold, crawling over rotted corpses, eyes missing, lips, toes and fingers missing, the bugs crunching on bone, my disrupted sleep leaving me lying in a puddle of sweat, feeling as if bugs and beetles and insects were crawling up my spine and burrowing into my skull, a most terrifying experience, one I hoped never to repeat.

#

During those early days, the majority of the crew, enigmas all, more often than not conveyed indifference toward me, the exceptions being O'Grady and Cook, the others treating me as if I were some oddity found at the zoo, something to be trifled with or simply ignored.

Under Cook's tutelage, I was schooled in the art of superstitions,

166

his constant nattering interrupting my thoughts as we made the preparations with regard to the evening meal, more fish stew, boiled carrots and mashed potatoes in addition to the stale bread. The one superstition I found most confusing—avoid redheads for they would bring bad luck, and yet, there was Captain Jacques, ginger-headed himself. Cook pooh-poohed the concept, telling me, 'We be thinkin' of him as having the colouring of a Viking, the size of the man, his strength. There be no bad luck with the captain at the helm.' Other superstitions included crossing paths with manta rays for it was well-known they would pull a ship under, the crew destined to a watery grave, a cat thrown overboard would bring death, which made me think perhaps my safety was paramount given my nickname, and the demise of a swallow or albatross, woe be our downfall.

Many a downfall also included the cruelty inflicted by the men on each other, often at meal time, squabbling over portion size and leftovers. Following one such argument, it was alleged a shifty-eyed fellow by the name of Rounder McPhee, he having lost an eye during childhood due to some unfortunate accident, stole a necklace from a fellow mate, a Michaelmas gold cross. Three of the crew chased McPhee about the deck, the remainder of the men whooping and hollering like a pack of hyenas, McPhee wide-eyed with terror, the one good-seeing eye, whilst he endeavored to steer clear of capture. He sprang to the mizzenmast and climbed the rigging, much like a monkey, the men after him, their blood boiling, seeking retribution.

Once caught, the necklace was found upon McPhee's person, the man too stupid to have hidden it away in some secure spot unbeknownst to the others. The quartermaster, under the direction of Captain Jacques, ordered McPhee strung up by his thumbs, his toes barely touching the deck, tap-dancing about like a great marlin pulled from the deep and hung from the mizzenmast. He dangled there for more than two hours, in agony. Unable to listen to his plaintive cries, imploring his shipmates to free him, the sound of it filling my very soul with heartbreak and grief, I took myself below, thinking McPhee's capture and subsequent wailings reminded me of myself, Moggy, a pitiful creature with no hope of escape.

In hindsight, to have witnessed such cruelty should not have come as a surprise, for the men were of different nationalities with different beliefs; some English, others Welsh, a few Dutch, another from French Guiana and the largest of the crew, a massive Russian, he being the master carpenter originally from the seaport of Vladivostok. Altercations arose, either by design or demand, a disparaging look, the accusation, cheating at cards, a crude remark made about someone's familial lineage, of which details, I shall not record, being the good Christian that I am. Other fights broke out during a game of backgammon or mahjong which resulted in the board overturned in anger, tiles upset and spilling upon the deck planking, many a tile lost in a crack or a crevice, never to be seen again.

I saw nosebleeds, broken noses, broken fingers, teeth kicked loose from a dislocated jaw while another, with their knee shattered, lay on the deck moaning like a child, and yet, much of the time, Jacques said nothing, failing to intervene. He told me later, 'If they be resorting to fisticuffs such as wee children in order to settle a score, I be leaving them be, so long as they be ready with flintlock and cutlass when the need be there.'

As to when that need would arise, I had no knowledge, the vast expanse of the ocean looking much like liquid phosphorous, us somewhere in the China Sea, islands in the distance, most probable the Okinawa Island chain known for its many coves rife with sandy beaches. Given the time of year, we sometimes saw fogbanks on the horizon due to the fact the weather was influenced by the warm cyclone currents, much seaweed, barnacles and kelp to be dealt with, the men lowering themselves over the sides of the vessel to clear away the debris.

As for fish and crustaceans, plenty abounded in the waters: mackerel, herring, lizard fishes and prawns. When the weather cooperated, Cook made use of such fishing which added greatly to the dishes he drummed up, more often than not, something from nothing, all of it looking and tasting much like boiled hash, not fit for a dog, but no one complained.

There were also days I read from the Bible, most notably Psalms which Captain Jacques quite enjoyed. He was especially fond of David and had me read time and again: 'Oh, my God, I trust in thee: let me not be ashamed, let not mine enemies triumph over me.' If only I too could have availed myself of such triumph—my freedom—but alas, that was not meant to be.

To be, was my teaching the captain basic penmanship whilst he strove to know more about the finer points, the flourishes and finesse of such a craft. We dove into that once he had a handle on the reading, of which I neither knew nor understood if he had indeed been trifling with me, all of it meant as entertainment, often spending many a long hour whereby he practiced over and over, having procured pen, paper and ink in copious amounts, showing me his day's labours as it progressed in its finery, expecting praise much like a school boy. To this day, I still do not know from whence any of those writing materials came. Stolen, I would imagine.

#

A month into our travels, I often saw pods of dolphins keeping abreast with the ship, curious and comical creatures as they crested the waves, their fluke-like tails pushing them forward with such strength, such maneuverability, their speed was incredible. I thought of my forced servitude, certain my wife would be resolved to the idea I was dead and gone, and what was she to do? My only hope, she had not sought passage back to England, not yet, still waiting on word as to what might have befallen me.

Then came a day when one of the men by the name of Mortimer Copley suffered a ruptured hernia having wrestled his opponent into submission, a fight over some indiscretion made at the other's expense, the exertion of the fight resulting in Copley's injury. I knew there to be no relief from such a misfortune even as I endeavored to push the perforated bulge back between his groin muscle wall, the man crying out in agony, his legs pulled up, his body writhing in pain.

With the help of Cook, we two tightly bound Copley in a sleeve-like bandage, my prognosis, sepsis would soon set in, due to his injury. That most grievous of infections began shortly after, brought on by a tear in his bowel, the poor devil suffering, his groans like that of a sick and dying animal. A week later, death claimed the poor chap, he laying on his bunk, never to rebound, moaning through the last of it as his life drained away. Captain Jacques ordered Copley's body to be sewn into a piece of tattered canvas, and presently, with his feet weighted down by two cannon balls, the dead man was slipped into the sea to join Davy Jones' locker, all of it completed in due course without pomp, circumstance nor ceremony, not a biblical word of comfort offered up on behalf of the man.

Then it was I who suffered a most debilitating affliction, that of loose bowels, possibly rancid butter which had gone through me like water, this happening two days following Copley's death, the experience filling me with fear. Never had I been so ill as I sprang from the lower bunk and grabbed a wooden bucket, endeavoring to hurry forth from the cabin to deal with my misfortune, having soiled myself. Cook hollered after me, 'Squeeze your butt cheeks, you filthy wench, or I be throwin' you overboard! The stench of you turns my stomach!'

I'd not suffered the pangs of seasickness since the night of my capture, having quickly found my sea legs, but now, woe was me, not at all able to stand for the dizziness prevailing. Cook took pity whilst chastising my predicament, helping me topside, speaking of the foul matter to no one, not even the captain, showing a side of him I had not deemed possible, something almost like compassion.

Cook's proper name was Michal Stanislaw, an apprentice blacksmith made jobless due to the death of his benefactor, originally from Blackpool. As a child of three, his family emigrated from Poland to the British Isles. We shared a bunk attached to the galley, Cooky, as the captain called him, the one to have provided me with a serviceable sailor's blouse and britches following my ordeal, my own clothing worn to shreds by this time, which meant any desire to rid myself of the stench of barnacles and fish had become a moot point.

There was, in addition to the assorted paraphernalia hung about the walls: boots, shirts, suspenders, a cooking ladle, a copper pot, also a bramble of pussy willows knotted into a wee ball and hung above Cook's top bunk, his belief in a Polish tale, that of kittens saved from drowning by the willows, one tree dipping its branches into the creek and thus the pussy willow came to wear a portion of the kittens fur ladened upon its buds, the kittens having clamored up the branches to safety, the tree thus named.

During our time together, Cook shared the histories of those aboard the Leviathan made jobless with the enactment of the

170

Cardwell Reforms some twenty years prior, the goal to abolish the purchase of officers' commissions and thereby end profiteering.

'What was a chap to be doin'?' he said. 'There was Captain Jacques, an outcast, stripped of his commission by them highfaluting politicians, in possession of the Leviathan. Since that time, we've plied the waters of the Indian Ocean and even made our way to the Americas. But the captain, he be fond of the China Sea and here we be, a hearty crew, loyal unto each other, and to Captain Jacques.'

Another fine evening, Cook relayed a story about a band of merry minstrels brought on board, jolly good fellows of which none spoke a morsel of the Queen's English. 'They was a sight to see, by gosh 'n golly, the way they be climbing,' he said.

This night we were sharing a wee dram of rum; the captain having given leave for all aboard to partake in such merriment. 'Two of the little devils scampered topside to the mizzenmast much like they was takin' a stroll in the park,' said Cook. 'And then, one standing on the shoulders of the other, seventy feet above the waves, out comes the knives, and they begin a'jugglin', three knives apiece. We'd never seen such a thing.'

Cook then said the minstrels came from the court of the Empress Dowager Cixi of the Quing dynasty, them too shanghaied, all meant for entertainment. 'The Dowager was there when they arrested and tortured that British diplomat, Harry Parkes. That be happening during the Second Opium War. You must'a heard of it.'

I nodded, myself no more than a child at the time, but my employer knew of it, knew of the arrest and torture of Harry Parkes, and there were times he fretted such an ending would befall him, and possibly all British citizens working and living in Shanghai, should the political tide shift its current position from friend to foe.

Presently there came singing from up on deck. 'Blow the man down, bullies, blow the man down, way hey, blow the man down.' I listened, a deep melancholy within my breast, wondering if there would ever truly come a day when I would set my feet upon dry land once more.

#

One afternoon when we'd taken a break from the studies, Captain

Jacques spoke of his many spies, a network on both land and at sea. 'There be a province in central China whereby the poor devils be treated no better than slaves,' he said. 'A sad lot, some crippled and blind, scrabbling about in the dirt like mangy dogs, leaving me filled with pity for the poor filthy beggars. When our paths cross, I have a middleman, much like your place of business, and he be delivering silver coins to be divided equally amongst the families what allows them to purchase rice and other items necessary to afford them some sense of wellbeing, the authorities none the wiser.'

'You? Offering an act of charity?'

'And why not, my good fellow? I be not all bad,' he said. 'I be neither a scoundrel nor a murderer. I'll be having you know, all of my exploits, nothing but flummery, tales given to newspaper men plying the seven seas, a lucrative term bestowed upon us by the Greeks, others writing those penny dreadfuls ever sought after by the commonfolk. We be attacking no one. We simply go from port to port, cove to cove, as the wind blows, playing hide 'n seek with the British admiralty, taking on fresh water, poultry, porridge, spirits and beer.' He laughed, finding much pleasure having made sport of me.

'But you went from profiteering to piracy, Cook has told me so,' I said. 'You were given a commission with the royal navy, subsequently abolished by our government, the politicians turning a blind eye. You mean it's all a falsehood?'

'Every last word, Moggy. It be the stuff of fairytales, my crew and I, flying the Jolly Roger.'

'And your fairytales will see you shot, or hanged, or both. You and your crew. What be the sense of that?' Dear Lord! I'd fallen into the trap, now speaking his vernacular!

'Posterity,' he said. 'What else were we to be doing? Once my commission was robbed from me, it be my Quartermaster, Jacob Cutter who devised the plan. We would be sowing the seeds of many a story, which would then be growing with each telling, the making of us. And nary a shot fired. Aye, me bucko, we be in cahoots with legitimate buccaneers. They be our mates, every one of them, sharing their booty with this band of misfits. As for us, we be providing the entertainment, that of the telling of the tales.'

So sublime in the telling was he that he almost had me believing him. But I'd seen once too often his mistreatment of the men: Dirty

172

Dan whipped for insubordination. Salty Dog beaten for stealing food. Cut-throat Carruthers locked in a cage in the ship's cargo deck for three days, denied water nor sustenance, the captain taking no initiative at the time of the offence, the discipline handed out days later. 'And yet, you have treated some of your crew with abject horror,' I stated. 'What of McPhee, the poor devil made to suffer. And the likes of Copley?'

'Even the most notable of school children must be disciplined,' he said. 'Especially when they be taking on airs or stealing. As for Copley, fate intervened, that which will befall each of us in due course and time. As for the others, I'll be having no theft nor cheating aboard this fine vessel, not unless it be done by me. A captain does, after all, have his prerogatives.'

#

As to never firing a shot, if there were some truths in that regard during my time aboard the Leviathan, there came a day we again spotted many shorebirds flying in a circle, gulls and terns, obviously something on the horizon having caught their attention. A call from on high informed all below, the birds circled above a ship, giving away its position.

Captain Jacques, standing on the quarterdeck, hollered, 'Heave-ho, my hearties. We've plunder to attend.' That morning, he'd dressed in attire more ostentatious than any I'd witnessed previously, a premonition perhaps, a foretelling in a dream? Cook would certainly have said so.

Jacques wore red velvet britches and an elaborate gold brocade coat, wide satin cuffs on the sleeves of his garment, the coat decorated with brass buttons and trimmed in Leopard skin, his tricorn hat sporting a peacock feather, the grandest I'd ever seen. I'd heard the stories extolling the plunders of Black Bart, Calico Jack and the most notorious of all, Blackbeard, all bearing down on ships without a shot fired, merchant marines surrendering their bounty. Jacques also looked a man of distinction, and very much a pirate captain, two flintlock pistols cushioned in a cloth sleeve, the sleeve wrapped about his chest, a cutlass strapped to his side.

Presently, the Leviathan was plowing through the surf with such speed I thought my eyes would spring forth from their sockets. A plan formed in my mind.

Whilst the men scurried to 'n fro making fast the sails and the jib fastened to the bowsprit, all done with much shouting and vigor, Jacques turned to me, 'I know what you be thinking, Moggy, my good man.' His eyes, hard as flint bore into my own whilst the corners of his lips curled in what was meant for a smile. 'I bid you to remember that with which I stated when you came aboard. You speak of your misfortune, alluding to kidnap, and I be making sport of your good wife. Of that I speak well and true.'

Presently, a vessel came in sight, its sails catching the sunlight, the ship lit up like the Holy Grail plying the waves. Under different circumstances she may have been able to outrun the Leviathan, but not this day, the Jolly Roger flapping in the wind, its signal as menacing as the captain standing on her quarterdeck, both with formidable reputations.

'Hey-ho, my hearties,' shouted Jacques. 'You be setting out on an early morning tide I expect, thinking to make a run for Taipei Shih, and here we be.' He laughed, his belly rippling with glee. 'What say you? We relieve you of your cargo, thereby making your load lighter, and you be buoyed upon the waves such as a wee babe in a basket.'

Captain Jacques' men cheered at that comment, waving cutlasses and flintlocks about like party toys. The merchant marines on the vessel HMS Achilleas, an eight-gun schooner, stood there meek as spring lambs.

'We'll not fight,' hollered their captain. 'Aye, we be bound to Taipei Shih with the Queen's mail, oils and herbs. What kind of a booty is that for you?'

'Booty, indeed,' hollered Captain Jacques in return. 'I expect you be carrying diplomatic pouches, government dispatch not meant for another's eyes.'

The captain of the HMS Achilleas flushed white as new fallen snow; the blood blanched right out of him, possibly believing it was better to have saved the ship and the lives of his men, the cargo insured, but now, what fate would await him? Important documents stolen at sea.

'Oh ho, my lads, a fine bounty we collect this day,' shouted Jacques.

His crew swung from ropes and grappling hooks and presently began the offloading without a single drop of blood shed, confirming Jacques' reputation boded him well, known to the navy and to others who plied the China seas, meaning the HMS Achilleas' fate was doomed from the start, as was mine, him having arrested any escape plan on my part due to the threat made against my wife, and me, falling mute as to my forced servitude, no rescue to be made this day by the likes of the captain of the HMS Achilleas, he too a victim of Jacques' cunning.

#

Two months to the day following my ordeal, Jacques called me to his cabin, once again sitting in that infernal chair on casters, rolling slightly to the left, then slightly to the right, the hinges in desperate need of an oiling.

'Your time with us be coming to an end Rupert Bartholomew Rey, spelled R-e-y.' He fussed with the ruffled cuffs on his shirt, setting the cuffs in place. 'And count your blessings you saw neither bloodshed nor violence whilst on board this fine vessel. You will be returned to your loved ones unscathed by neither illness nor injury. I should be thinking you would be thanking Cooky and me for having taken such good care of you.'

Cook obviously had not shared with him that terrible bout I'd suffered with the loose bowels. 'You call what I have endured these past two months care? My clothing reeks with the stench of barnacles and fish. My beard too long, my skin weathered by the wind and the rain, and sun damage.'

The fact I'd not been allowed the use of a razor for there were none on board, shouldn't have come as a surprise, the crew believing if they were to cut their hair or their nails, or shave, grief would befall all those aboard the Leviathan. Far be it from me to push the matter. Cook had further informed me numerous times, should I fall overboard, I would indeed be left to the fishes, my death preordained, what the sea wants, the sea shall have.

Now here was the captain referencing the man who'd been my keeper. 'Cooky tells me, you be a splendid fellow, full of questions to which he has regaled you with many a fine tale of adventure,

175

entertainment for entertainment's sake.'

'A monkey on a string,' I said.

'Even monkeys have their use,' he said, laughing and slapping a knee, the beads jangling in his plaited beard. He then handed me a document, penned by him, his script flourishing in all its finery, a handful of spelling mistakes but nothing which detracted from the content.

The Last Will and Testament of Captain Jacques Soho, born in the city of Bristol, taken to sea at the age of eight by his uncle, lost to the sea much as Job was lost, swallowed by the great whale. 'This be the reason for my capture? You could have dictated this to anyone who has the ability to read and write. You need not have shanghaied me into service.'

'Ah, but my dear Moggy, how would I ever be knowing that which I dictated was well and true? Whoever be doing the writing, they could have hoodwinked me, any old word scribbled on parchment, and me none the wiser. I have done that which I desired.' He sat back, grinning, much like the boy who cried wolf, making sport of the townspeople. 'Is it not a splendid rendering of a Last Will and Testament, incorporating all that you have taught me?'

I glanced again at the document, taking note he'd bequeathed his worldly possessions to someone named Persephone Josephina Soho. 'Your daughter?' I asked. 'Or perhaps a wife?'

'My sister, in Bristol,' he said. 'She be married to a seafaring man. I never did learn me his name, but scuttlebutt has it, she bore three children, two lads and a lassie.'

His grin faded as he stroked his plaited beard. 'I be dying, Moggy. That knowledge was given to me many months ago by a physician brought on board, shanghaied much like yourself. A malignant growth that's been festering over time, nothing to be done.' He tapped his skull, just behind his right ear. 'Here, it be something in the brain, the reason I do not eat, do not sleep. The reason I be avoiding the rum, the tobacco, it having nothing to do with Puritanical beliefs, what some of the crew have surmised. The reason for the terrible headaches, the slurring of my words. The pain now be constant, threatening to hinder me in my duties, bedeviling me, something I cannot allow the men to know.'

I was dumbfounded. He'd never so much as twinged a muscle nor wrinkled a brow nor twisted his face in pain. 'You bear it well,' I stated.

'To be showing any sign of weakness, I'd soon be a dead man, and I be not ready for death, not yet, this final duty to perform. I be leaving this document in your care. Once you return home, it be your duty to settle my affairs. There be silver enough to hire good legal counsel, coins aplenty when you depart the ship. I trust you will be negotiating a respectable transaction, a buyer who will appreciate the finer attributes of this vessel for she be of a sound heart and a sturdy disposition. Your commission, ten percent of her value as payment as Executor, and then, you be seeing that the remainder is forwarded to my sister.'

'It's as simple as that, is it? Someone you have not seen since you were a child.'

'Persephone was the only one to do me a kindness,' he said, his eyes taking on a faraway gaze into some past memory of which I knew naught. 'If there be such a thing as love, I have always held her in high regard. If you should be learning that she herself, be dead, then ensure that my legacy is divided equally amongst her heirs, that which by default would thus be mine.'

There it was, his cards laid upon the table. 'A pirate's life I have led,' he continued, 'but that does not mean I cannot be ending it in a gentlemanly fashion.'

'Well, I'll be,' and I said no more, tucking the document into an oilskin pouch, one he'd handed to me, keeping it safe within the folds of my blouse. 'When shall I be put ashore?'

'Tomorrow,' he said. 'We be but a hare's breath off the coast of Hangzhou Bay. We'll be taking advantage of a neap tide, the waters calm, the weather fair. From there, you being an able-bodied man, you should be having no trouble making your way to Shanghai. Any reputable seaman could make that journey in three days, blindfolded. Avail yourself of a donkey cart should you be needing it. There is bound to be a farmer who could provide such a thing, perhaps a son to escort you.'

He then laughed and smacked his thigh. 'I be hearing you conversing with Cooky, telling him you spoke a form of pidgin Mandarin. It now be your turn to make yourself understood. Any monies spent on transport is to be coming from your pocket as

Executor, see to that. I do not want you to skimp on that which goes to my sister.'

'You would put your trust in me,' I said. 'Who is to say I would not simply destroy the document, no one the wiser? Or if I am waylaid by bandits, they may take the paper from me.'

'Should you be doing such a thing, I will know,' he responded forthwith, his eyes again filled with malevolence, that thing I saw so often these past two months. 'As I have told you, I have spies everywhere, all loyal to me. How else do you be thinking I have the ability to pillage the seas, ravage coastal villages, all without the authorities set upon me. Think of me as a God.'

'And even Gods must fall,' I said.

'And die, my fine fellow. And die. Zeus, Poseidon, Aphrodite, even Apollo, all dead and lost to the history books. You be showing me that.'

'You too shall be lost to the history books,' I countered, giving him a mock salute, clicking my heels together as though he were something of a pretend naval officer, one attached to the British admiralty, the perceived scoundrel that he was. I then surmised, his had been a lonely life, his mistresses that of the sea, his vessel, and his booty, others brought on board as a mere distraction, their roles to entertain.

Despite his claim to innocence or infamy, I remained mute with regard to his Last Will and Testament, he surely in the know such a document would be deemed null and void by any reputable court of the land due to the fact his story as an innocent seafarer would never have been believed. As to the spinning of his tales alluding to the concept he was something of a Robin Hood—stealing from the rich, giving to the poor—I reckoned there were many witnesses to the contrary, whether they'd be giving false testimony or not, stating he was a renegade flying the Jolly Roger, and thereby a criminal in the eyes of the law. It was common knowledge the British navy commanded the seas, all but wiping out piracy, their intent to rid the oceans of the vermin seeking to ruin commerce and trade, making the pirate life the stuff of legend and ballads. Pirates were indeed a dying breed, in more ways than one. The fact that Captain Jacques had lived this long was something of a miracle in and of itself.

He must surely know that I, a mere secretary, would never be allowed an opportunity to lay my hands upon his vessel nor his treasure, should the news come that he was indeed deceased. His crew would elect a new captain and carry on with their plunder, Jacques' booty divvied up amongst the men until they too ran afoul of the greatest fleet the world had ever known.

Neither his sister nor her heirs would see a farthing of Jacques' riches.

#

The following day, I did not see him. The bo'sun and another rowed me ashore without a word spoken, steering clear of the tidal bore whilst bringing the ship's launch parallel to the muddy beach along the northern edge of Hangzhou Bay. I rolled up my pantlegs and set forth, wading knee-deep through the tide. I'd been given a small chest filled with silver, easily within my means to carry, the weight of it no more than a twenty-pound cannon ball. They then rowed back to the Leviathan, a vessel I was never to see again, my prayers sent heavenward, thanking our Heavenly Father, whether he be Jewish, Catholic, Protestant or Greek for allowing me once again to set my feet upon terra firma whilst setting my sights toward home.

During those travels, I often wondered if Jacques lived in a kind of theatre of the mind, not in the guise of a dress rehearsal but the actual performance heightened by audience participation, whether that audience be shanghaied or not, he and his men living the life of the buccaneer, the stuff of fairytales. To that end, I would never know, for the morning I arrived in Shanghai following three days of arduous travel just as Jacques had stated, having bribed many an official with the silver in an effort to attain safe passage, I was met at my place of business by an elderly Chinese gentleman hobbling along with stick and cane, the man crippled with injury, one of Jacques paid spies, I surmised. He carried with him the message, Captain Jacques Soho was dead, his body found floating amongst the flotsam and jetsam in Hangzhou Bay, a flintlock in one hand, a cutlass in the other, ever the swashbuckler, one of the last of his kind to hoist the Jolly Roger, now gone to meet his maker on his own terms, beholden to no one.

# AUTHOR BIOGRAPHIES

**Lawrence Dagstine** is a native New Yorker, video game enthusiast, toy collector, and speculative fiction writer of 25+ years. He has placed close to 500 short stories in online and print periodicals during that two-decade plus span, especially the small presses. He has been published by publishing houses such as Damnation Books, Steampunk Tales, Left Hand Publishers, Wicked Shadow Press, and Dark Owl Publishing (of which he has a new book out called *The Nightmare Cycle*). He is also the author of two story collections, *Death of the Common Writer* and *Fresh Blood.*
*lawrencedagstine.com*

**Paulene Turner** is a writer of short stories, short plays, and novels. Her short stories have appeared in magazines and anthologies in the UK, US, and Australia. As well as writing short plays, she also directs them for Short and Sweet, Sydney—the biggest little play festival in the world. She lives in Sydney with her husband, twin daughters, and twin pugs, Holmes and Watson.
*pauleneturnerwrites.com*

**Michael Fountain** has worked as a fruit picker, diaper service laundryman, psychiatric aide, bartender, and schoolteacher in both urban and rural settings. His short story "Buddy Bolden's Last Stand" appears in the print anthology *Uncommon Minds*. A comedy, *Trojan War Confidential*, has been staged in the U.S. and Canada and is available from Brooklyn Publishers. His non-fiction has appeared in several regional magazines.
*michaelfountain.blogspot.com*

**S. B. Watson** lives in Keizer, Oregon. His stories have appeared in Spinetingler Magazine, Mystery Tribune, The Dark City Mystery Magazine, Punk Noir Magazine, Mystery Magazine, and JayHenge's *The Back Forty* anthology.
*sbwatson.com*

**Jack Wells** is a burgeoning author located in Northern Utah. He has been writing on and off since grade school, though most of his early works consist of bad poetry and even worse song lyrics. Some of his more serious writing experience includes penning amateur reviews of movies, novels (multiple genres), and video games for various websites.
*facebook.com/jack.wells.969*

**Edward Lodi** has written more than thirty books, both fiction and non-fiction, including six Cranberry Country Mysteries. His short fiction and poetry have appeared in numerous magazines and journals, such as Mystery Magazine, and in anthologies published by Cemetery Dance, Murderous Ink, Main Street Rag, Rock Village Publishing, Superior Shores Press, and others. His story, *Charnel House*, was featured on Night Terrors Podcast. He is a member of the Short Mystery Fiction Society and a frequent contributor to their blog.

**Rose Biggin** is a writer and performer based in London. Her short fiction has appeared in various anthologies and made the recommended reading list for Best of British Fantasy; her first short fiction collection is forthcoming from NewCon Press. She is the author of two novels: punk fantasy *Wild Time* (Surface Press) and gothic thriller *The Belladonna Invitation* (Ghost Orchid Press), and is an associate lecturer in Creative Writing at Birkbeck. Twitter: @rosebiggin

**Cameron Trost** is an author of mystery, suspense, horror, and post-apocalyptic fiction. He is best known for his puzzles featuring Oscar Tremont, Investigator of the Strange and Inexplicable. He has written three novels, *Flicker, Letterbox* and *The Tunnel Runner*, and three collections, *Oscar Tremont,*

*Investigator of the Strange and Inexplicable*, *The Animal Inside*, and *Hoffman's Creeper and Other Disturbing Tales*. Originally from Brisbane, Australia, Cameron lives with his wife and two sons near Guérande in southern Brittany, between the rugged coast and treacherous marshland. He runs the independent publishing house, Black Beacon Books, and is a member of the Australian Crime Writers Association.
*camerontrost.com*

**Karen Bayly** began writing as a child when she wrote soap operas for her dolls to perform under her creative direction. These days it's her biology PhD, research background, and general dismay at the way the world is going that informs her writing, a fusion of science fiction, horror, and fantasy. She lives in the outer suburbs of Sydney, Australia, with two cats, a guitar, and a ukulele.
*karenbayly.com*

**DJ Tyrer** is a writer, poet, and the person behind Atlantean Publishing, as well as having been the non-fiction editor for Redsine in 2000/01 and co-editor of the two-part *King in Yellow* special of Cyaegha in 2014/15. Publication credits include a variety of anthologies, small press magazines, gaming magazines, chapbooks, two novellas and more. DJ Tyrer has worked in education, administration, retail, management and public relations and currently resides in Southend-on-Sea, Essex, England, UK.
*djtyrer.blogspot.com*

**Karen Keeley** has published short fiction in more than a dozen anthologies: literary, speculative and crime. Recent stories appear in *An Ancient Curse Vol. II* (PulpCult publisher, an imprint of CultureCult Press) and *Tales from the Monoverse* (Last Waltz Publishing). As a kid, she read *Treasure Island* and *Robinson Crusoe* (who didn't?), enthralled with the lives of buccaneers, those randy rouges who made mockery of others while plundering their wealth. She didn't grow up to be a bandit. She does however, still enjoy pirate tales with their swashbuckling savoir faire.
*karenmkeeley.blogspot.com*

## Also Available from Black Beacon Books
Our inaugural anthology of horror tales!

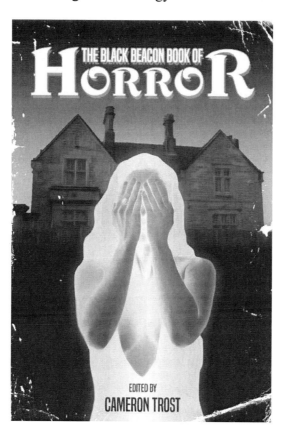

**For news, reviews, competitions, author interviews, and exclusive excerpts**

**Visit our website**
blackbeaconbooks.com

**Like us on Facebook**
facebook.com/BlackBeaconBooks

**Join us on X**
@BlackBeacons

**Find us on Instagram**
instagram.com/blackbeaconbooks

**Subscribe on Patreon**
patreon.com/blackbeaconbooks

**Discover All our Social Media Links**
https://linktr.ee/blackbeaconbooks